NATIONAL EMERGENCY

National Emergency

By
James Jobling

Back Road Books

Published in Great Britain in 2015 by
Back Road Books
Manchester, UK

Acknowledgements

Where do I begin with this?

From the wretched first draft to the finished article you're holding, I faced a lot of demons during the writing of this book (and thanks to my son, I had to write the whole thing on a laptop with no T, M, or Backspace button). Sometimes it really was like banging my head against a brick wall. I can't remember the amount of times I've considered throwing the entire thing in the bin and starting over. Thanks to the people below, I didn't.

Sean Page, thank you for wedging a size 10 Doctor Marten up my backside and getting me back into writing again. No matter how many times I badgered you, you always had time for me. I really appreciate that.

Huge thanks to Jeremy Peterson for not only being a genuinely nice guy but for proofreading my work and putting the blurb on my cover. His debut novel, A Devil in God's Country, will be available April, 2015.

Sincere special thanks to Adam Millard and Robert Robinson, and to all of my fellow Survivors in the Facebook Wander in the Aftermath circle for their continued support; especially Rich Hawkins, Calum Chalmers, Nat Robinson, Charlie Morgan, Jason Fowler, and Paige Topinka. I would like to take this opportunity to wish you all the best of luck with your future endeavours. David Moody you are, and continue to be, my influence – and we even share the same dreadful taste in movies.

To my beautiful wife Trish thanks for putting up with me and supporting me through the completion of this book. I told you we'd get there. I know its cliché, but you're my rock, mother to my two gorgeous (sleep-avoiding) babies, and you deserve to be showered with praise for everything you have, and continue, to go through. We WILL get you better.

Chase, Amelia, Daddy's Little Smashers, I love you more than words can describe. This one is for you two.

Bring it on.

James Jobling.

Foreword

When it comes down to it, me and this Jobling guy didn't have the once chance encounter that most writers have. From the moment I first met him and embarrassed myself by pressing him with a trust exercise question, I thought he was a right prick. And I'm sure you'll not gasp or giggle when I tell you after ten years that opinion still stands!

It was back when I was an artist that myself and this Jobling guy started talking about stories and such. He explained the ideas he had with such detailed visuals and with a film director like precision, which wowed me with his ability to give you the amazing mental image of exactly what he wanted you to see. And then there was me. I was/am the kind of guy who'll only ever gush to myself...with you only being there in earshot, hearing me go on about "It'll have this...and then this happens...then this girl, with this power, can jump and maim and slash, and so on and so on and, you know...on.

But, where my mind lays in the realm of awkward perversions (let's give that an oo-er), this Jobling guy's mind lays in the parallel realm of true urban darkness...a place in the mind even myself and my twisted soul are too scared to tread. His ideas come from the one horrible patch of grey matter that deals with a part of the world that I do my very best to avoid, to the point of shutting it out almost completely. And that is the realm of Reality.

National Emergency revolves around a piece of this Reality that, like many of us, I have no idea what part of the brain creates such actions. Feeling angry is one thing, but the whole act of rioting seems to me a little like cutting off your nose to spite your face. Much like the poor gentleman who set himself on fire to prevent the tanks from advancing, as truly tragic as that was, if I was going to do something to somebody to get a point across, I wouldn't walk out of my house, pick up a brick, spin on my heel s and proceed to smash my neighbours windows, or run to a random person's store and steal from them, because neither yourself nor the random person with the store has anything to do with why you're rioting. Damaging and hurting everyone and everything BUT the people you are angry at doesn't seem all that intelligent to me. Then again, on the stat rolling INT was a critical miss during their creation. Am I right? Up top? No?

The thing is, this Jobling guy's brilliant writing has made me enjoy a story based on a genre that I am not comfortable with. And, as odd as it feels to say/write, I want to see how much further into his darkness he can go, and experience the Hell he felt that caused him to write this.

Jake Oldroyd author of **BOUNCE CITY**

Prologue

The pain was unbearable. She had been in labour for over eleven hours, straight through the night; her anxious husband beside her every step of the way. He was silently going to pieces, but determined to remain strong for her, his nerve unwavering. As dawn broke on another bleak and rainy morning, the baby's head engaged and the power of the contractions pushed it deeper into her pelvis.

An hour and a half later – after thirty-five weeks of pregnancy – the midwife placed a beautiful son onto his mother's chest. Pregnancy had been strenuously exhausting, the labour itself a torturous misery which had discouraged both parents from further children, but he was finally here, naked, squirming, smeared with blood and vernix, screaming his tiny lungs up his tiny gullet. Their son had finally arrived. The father had blubbered as the midwife had congratulated him for surviving such a challenging night (she had been convinced he was going to pass out during the epidural) and then a nurse swaddled the baby in a clean towel and capped his head with a hat.

The midwife clamped and carved the umbilical cord, severing it from the placenta and then, with mother and son locking eyes and falling in love, the nurse rushed the baby into assessment. The husband mopped his wife's forehead with kisses, reassuring her, thanking her, slipping out of the delivery suite to ring his mother as further contractions made his wife give birth for the second time, evicting the placenta from her gaping womb.

Inside the warming unit, the newborn's nose and mouth were suctioned and his heart rate and muscle response tested. After being weighed, the nurse pierced the skin of the baby's thigh with a syringe and thumbed the plunger down, administering a clear fluid into the screaming baby. The injection was placed on the side as the child was wrapped up once more in the towel and carried back out to his delighted parents.

A burly porter, his green overalls barely restraining his massive stomach, smiled cheerfully at the new parents as they were wheeled past him into recovery. He quickly began the task of picking up bloody bed sheets and sodden towels, disposing of them in his cart, pushing open the swinging doors leading into the assessment unit. He hated this part of the job. No, he despised it! He scratched unnecessarily at his bald head and held the injection between his podgy thumb and forefinger. The words printed on the front of the pierced glass vial simply read TK-214. The porter shook his head and dropped the used syringe, along with the empty glass vial, into a waste bucket and began cleaning the room.

CHAPTER 1

For Christ's sake, I need this like I need a bullet in the head!

He recognized the two cars parked in his driveway as soon as he pulled up – his mother and her loser fiancés beaten-to-crap Ford and his brother and his dictator of a wife's Honda (which only two days ago, Lee had confided had not passed its MOT). Ethan Hardcastle sat for a few seconds and stared out of the windscreen, fingernails sinking into the hard leather of the steering wheel, praying to God, praying to Buddha, praying to whichever mystical entity was in charge of this spinning blue marble that what he was seeing was nothing more than a mirage brought on by the trauma of turning forty that morning. He even closed his eyes, silently wondering what had possessed Karris to mark the occasion with a gathering, and then blinked them open, heart deflating when he saw the two cars still parked there. He snatched off the engine with a weary sigh, and opened the door of his BMW Pickup, and stepped out. Gravel crunched noisily beneath the soles of his boots.

He stretched his broad back and thick arms, hearing the joints pop (a certification that he was indeed getting old) and stifled a yawn with a gloved hand. The Pickup was loaded with the timber required to begin work on the conservatory. Karris had been pestering him about it since the dawn of time, or so it seemed. He considered unloading before entering the house.

It'll only take a couple of minutes to stack in the corner of the garage. Plus, Nathan needs the Pickup empty for that job in Blackpool tomorrow.

The front door opened, however, before he had a chance, and his wife of the past eight years stepped into the porch, a bowl of salad under one arm and a worried scowl on her beautiful face.

Ethan pulled his short-sleeved shirt off and rolled it up, tossing it into the bed of lumber, and walked towards Karris with his hands on his hips and his head hung low. He ascended the two steps leading into the lattice framework encasing her and pecked her on the forehead, stepping back, nodding towards the two cars parked behind him.

"Please don't be mad, baby," she said. She pushed a hand through the waterfall of blonde hair gushing past her shoulders. She had her extensions in. He loved it when she wore her extensions. "Your Mum rang last week," she continued to babble, "said we should do something special for your fortieth. She wanted to throw you a surprise birthday party with all your family and friends; a cake, buffet, banners, balloons, a DJ, the whole shebang."

Ethan grunted. Something resembling a smile creased his stubbly features. "And how did you know that wasn't exactly what I want?"

She looked at him with puppy dog eyes, the little minx's lips pert. His gloved hands grabbed her petite waist, dusty fingers dirtying the white blouse compressing her breasts.

"Because, sweetheart, your idea of a good night is drinking a cold beer while your hot wife straddles you in bed." She leaned forward and gave him a generous glimpse of her colliding cleavage. He smiled widely.

"If you know this then why have you invited my mother over?"

She placed a finely-manicured hand on his sculptured chest, over his beating heart, grabbing a handful of his grubby vest. "It's only for a couple of hours, misery guts. And I've even invited a few of your drinking buddies 'round. Plus, if you're a really good boy, I will let you unwrap your present in the kitchen tonight."

"What is my present?" Ethan asked, liking the sound of where this was going.

"Me," she giggled. Tantalising fingers danced over the crotch of his jeans. She felt him go hard immediately.

Suddenly a police helicopter surged through the dreary clouds above, hovering momentarily over the bungalow as though the pilot was scrutinising the property below, running accusatory eyes over them, before soaring away into the gloomy heavens. Ethan stepped back and looked up into the sky, shielding his eyes with his hand from the burning orb. It wasn't your typical May evening; it was cloudy if anything, but the sun still sat dead-centre in the middle of the faded blue sky; proud, boastful, throbbing heat into a creeping night.

"I wonder what that's about," Ethan said.

Karris poked her head out and followed his gaze. "I don't know." She shifted the salad bowl from one arm to the other. "There was some trouble this morning."
Ethan's eyes narrowed.

"No, honey, I didn't mean here," Karris said. "A young black lad died in police custody. It's been all over the news today. He died of head trauma apparently, but the police are refusing to say how or what caused his death. They won't even release his body."

"What? That's just crazy," Ethan said. Blobs of black floaters danced insanely in front of his irises.

"I know. It's disgusting."

"I guess that explains why the M6 was backed up all the way to Macclesfield then."

She nodded and he entered the house, closing the front door behind him and untying his boots. He was no prude but the carpets were practically brand new and if he dirtied them now it'd cost a tiny fortune to hire a carpet-cleaner later. He walked along the hall leading into the front room, stopping before he'd properly begun, straightening an unbalanced frame containing a Superman comic. He had been an avid fan of comic books since childhood; a hobby at first, persisting through his teenage years, growing into a full-blown obsession by adulthood. His entire hallway was covered with original Marvel and DC framed treasures that he had purchased online or from eBay. It was something his friends repeatedly ribbed him about. Not that Ethan cared. To him, owning the very first edition of Batman or Spiderman and watching them develop into the multi-million pound franchises they were today was mesmerising. They had always been an unremitting presence through his early years; hours of endless pleasure created from nothing more than ink, speech bubbles, and natural talent. He was proud of his collection. One day his son Lincoln would inherit the lot. "Yeah," Karris said, derailing his train of thought. "The poor boy's family have called for a rally. They intend to march from Levine Square all the way into the city. The police are on the scene, keeping an eye on things and making sure nothing kicks off."

Ethan rolled his eyes.

"They have made it very clear that they have riot police at their disposal, too."
"Good thing," Ethan said. He nodded towards the closed door concealing his family. "We might need them."

CHAPTER 2

"Happy birthday, son,"

Ethan grimaced when he heard the familiar voice but the gesture went unseen due to the fact that he had his head ducked inside the refrigerator. He sighed jadedly, gripped a bottle of beer by the neck and pulled it free, slamming the door shut.
"Alright, Harry?"

Harold Singleton smiled crookedly. He was puffing on a roll-up, faint blue smoke wafting into the air. A bloated hand slipped through his shoulder-length dark hair. The greasy mop looked as though a shower hadn't fumigated it for months. When he spoke, the vile stench emanating from the man's mouth made Ethan want to bleach his nostrils.
"I can't complain," Harold said. He was nibbling on a chicken drumstick, and had clearly ignored the stack of paper napkins on the buffet table. Instead, he wiped his slippery fingers on the bottom of his Hawaiian shirt. "Well, I can complain," he continued, flashing yellow calcified thorns when he spoke, "but your bloody mother never listens."
Ethan placed the unopened bottle of beer on the draining board and propped himself up against the sink; head down, staring at the polished beams of his kitchen floor, hoping this little confrontation didn't linger on for too long. He didn't particularly hate his mother's fiancé. He didn't even dislike him. As far as Ethan knew, Harold treated his mother with as much respect and decorum as a former heroin addict could muster. He had never blacked her eye at least, or broken her nose, or put her in hospital because his tea wasn't on the table when he'd finally

returned from the pub. Which was more than could be said for his own father (not to mention the countless other law-breaking, heartbreaking bastards she'd dated over the years). There was no denying that Harold was a slob. For Harold Singleton, hanging around his bedsit all day drinking cheap beer, smoking cannabis, betting on horses, and being a general drain on society was a way of life. His mother could do better, a lot better, she deserved better, but that didn't make Harold a particularly bad person, did it? Ethan didn't think so. He folded his thick arms across his wide chest and continued to look down at the floor.

"How's business, son?" asked Harold. He placed the butt of the cigarette between his lips again and inhaled hard, relishing the suffocating goodness expanding within his lungs. Ethan gritted his teeth when ash dropped onto the carpet.

"Not bad, Harry," said Ethan. He refused point blank to make eye contact. "I've been up Macclesfield all week building a conservatory. The journey's a bitch but it pays the bills, right?" Ethan finally cracked open the beer and raised it to his parted lips. "What about you, Harry? Still looking for work?"

"The chance would be a fine thing, son," Harold said, chewing anxiously on an overgrown fingernail. "Back's still giving me gyp." He rested a hand against his spine and winced as he stretched. Second thoughts, you're not much different from my old man, after all.

"While we're on the subject of work," Harold said, taking a final hit on the cigarette and dropping it in an empty coffee mug on the side. Ethan inhaled a gust of frustrated oxygen up his nostrils and chewed manically on the insides of his mouth. "I was wondering if you could loan me twenty quid. Only until I get my giro at the end of the week. Gas and electric's off, you see? I was promised a windfall that didn't happen. Can you believe that?"

"No. I can't," Ethan answered.

"I'll pay you back; obviously, I just need a little something to see me and your mother through."

Ethan slipped a hand into the back pocket of his jeans and pulled out his wallet. He unclasped it and pulled two twenty pound notes free. He sighed once more and handed the money over to Harold, whose nicotine-caked fingers tried snatching the cash. Ethan held tightly on.

"Not for drugs, Harry."

Harold shook his head, virtually salivating.

"Thank you, son,"

"I'm not your fucking son."

Ethan released the money and Harold stuffed it into his grimy jeans. Smiling crookedly, he backed off as though he had just got his stinking hands on the Queen's Crown. Ethan shook his head and walked out of the room, leaving his mother's fiancé drooling over the money. Of course, he knew it'd be invested at the bookies later, but he didn't particularly care. He pushed open the door leading into the dining room and breathed a sigh of relief when he saw it was empty. A TV mounted to the wall was playing on mute. What he saw made his blood freeze.

News report: a newsreader in a city somewhere Ethan didn't recognize at first, but then he caught a glimpse of the neon-lit name of a nightclub called Fever, and he realized it was his city. Behind the newsreader a group of hooded youths were destroying a police car. They were throwing bricks and traffic cones and bins and slabs of concrete, everything at their disposal; ravaging, denting, humiliating the vehicle. A couple of troublesome teens had climbed onto the roof, cheering, stomping, kicking the flash bar free, jumping up and down on the spiderwebbed windscreen, damaging, wounding. Their hooded comrades surrounded the vehicle, shouldering it from both sides, bouncing it on its suspension, rocking it, trying to turn it over. There weren't any constables inside the car or anywhere in sight. Where were the police? The middle-aged announcer was standing in front of a jerky camera, microphone in hand and a worried expression etched on his face, jabbering on, but Ethan couldn't hear what he was saying because the TV was on mute. He glanced around for the remote control, eager to discover what was happening in his city, but he couldn't find it anywhere. Lincoln had an irritating habit of putting things in the bin. There was a headline in bold writing at the bottom of the screen which read: DENNISON ASARIA DEATH SPARKS RIOTS IN THE CAPITAL. There was a rolling caption beneath galloping across the screen, but it was sliding too fast for his tired eyes to pay any real attention to. He was about to step closer when the door behind him opened and Karris strolled in.

"Hey, handsome," she said, approaching him from behind and massaging his thick shoulders. He allowed his head to loll, his wife's thumbs manipulating deep muscles. He closed his eyes and drifted. "What are you doing in here alone, birthday boy?" She nibbled his earlobe.

"I'm just grabbing a breather."

She kissed the base of his neck, the tip of her tongue slurping a trail from his neck to his cheek, where she traded rough stubble for soft lips, kissing him passionately. Their tongues broke into each other's mouths, colliding, swapping juices. He pushed her roughly against the dining table, calloused hands grabbing her buttocks. "Honey," she breathed into the canal of his ear. "Do you want your present now?"
"What? Are you kidding?"

He tried pushing her away but, in truth, only a molecule of strength was actually used. "We can't do it here."

Her fingers expertly unbuttoned his jeans, releasing his stiff member and, seductively, she abseiled down his length, dropping provocatively to her knees. "Don't worry, if anybody walks in, I'll make sure they enjoy the show."
He groaned loudly.

Karris took him in her mouth.

Behind him, the police car erupted in a soundless ball of fire as a petrol bomb burst against the bonnet and baked the engine, detonating the vehicle.

CHAPTER 3

Ethan Hardcastle opened the door leading out of the dining room and stepped into the hall; red-faced, breathless, with perspiration drying on his skin. He looked over at Mike Lester, a life-long friend, and frowned when he saw him trying to console his sobbing girlfriend. He was stroking Emily's hair, kissing her forehead, promising her that they were going to be okay. The door behind Ethan creaked open and Karris crept out, disappearing quickly into the downstairs bathroom, eager to flush her mouth of the boiling hot ocean water she had just swallowed.

Ethan stepped beneath the archway and into the front room, wondering why his family and friends were standing in a circle around the coffee table, watching the plasma. Lee, his older brother – the second of three – was leaning against the wall and chewing robotically on a wedge of birthday cake. Crumbs were piling up on the carpet around his feet. He looked at his younger brother and cocked an eyebrow questioningly when he saw Karris close the bathroom door quietly, hair chaotic. Ethan nodded towards Mike and Emily and ignored his brother's sly smirk.

"What's going on?"

Lee thumbed the remainder of the cake into his mouth, chewing, swallowing, and speaking as though he had a mouthful of hot potato. "Something's kicked off in town. I knew it would. They're rioting over that black kid who died this morning."

"You mean Dennison Asaria?"

"Who's that?"

Ethan banished the question with a wave of his hand.

"Anyway, they're looting shops, fighting the police. Looks like the bloody Rodney King riots all over."

He crooked a thumb towards the TV where another news reporter was standing in front of a supermarket. The automatic doors leading into the store had been forced open and a horde of hooded youths were streaming inside, causing chaos, taking whatever they wanted. Ethan swallowed hard as he watched them ransacking the store, selecting what they wanted, shoving through the crowd, disappearing into the night. Ethan glanced nervously at his brother. His brain refused to absorb what his eyes were projecting back to it. The reporter continued jabbering into the microphone, a strong breeze whipping through his hair and jostling the sound of his voice. Behind him, a constant rivulet of hooded and balaclava-clad Neanderthals poured out, carrying boxes containing TVs, stereos, and computers. Ethan's ears picked out phrases such as "copycat behaviour" and "gang culture" repeatedly.
"This is insane," he breathed. He squeezed Lee's shoulder and walked into the front room, manoeuvring through the crowd. He found his mother and Harold sitting on the leather sofa, watching the news like a couple of Meerkats that had just spotted a line of juicy caterpillars.

"Mum," Ethan said. He crouched beside the sofa. "Are you okay?"
"There you are, sweetie. We couldn't find you. Harold looked all over. Have you seen what's happening in town, darling? They are vultures, absolute vultures!"
Ethan grabbed his mother's hand and stroked it, smiling reassuringly. "I know. But there's nothing to be afraid of.

They're just a couple of delinquents taking advantage of a situation."
The on-screen reporter was being advised by the studio panel to move away and find a more secure location to broadcast from. Ethan turned and looked at the TV just in time to see a gloved hand clasp over the lens and snatch the camera away.
"My God in Heaven!" his mother gasped. Her hands clutched the sides of her jowly face and her mouth hung open, cartoonish. "They just stole that camera!"
"Bloody mindless morons, the lot of 'em," Harold grunted, swigging from a can of lukewarm Guinness. "They're tearing their own bloody city apart."

"The police will regain control soon. There's nothing to worry about, Ma," said Ethan.

"I wouldn't be so sure about that." Harold smiled wickedly. "The cops have retreated completely out of the city."
"I'm sure they know what they're doing, Harry."

"What, the old Bill? Don't make me laugh, son."

Two bullets of pure anger were fired from Ethan Hardcastle's brown irises, shooting Harold Singleton down dead. "I'm sure they'll get the situation under control, right, Harry?"

"Oh yeah, sure thing," Harold replied, surprising the builder by holding his stare. "They've just got to dodge all those bricks and petrol bombs first."
Ethan rose to his feet, fingers curling into meaty fists. He opened his mouth to say something to the lush when Mike stepped forward. He was still consoling an obviously

distraught Emily.

“Hey,” Mike said, grabbing Ethan by the elbow and spinning him slowly. “Look, I’m really sorry mate, but we’re going to have to leave. Emily wants to check on her mum. Her house is right in the middle of town and she only began her chemo last week.”

“You’re going into town?” Harold asked, shaking his head and tsking loudly. “Not a wise move, my friend.”

“Yeah, well we don’t really have a choice,” Mike said, staring down at the drunken fossil, wiping tears from Emily’s flushed cheeks. Ethan stepped forward and draped an arm around Mike’s shoulders, leading him towards the front door. He had only just opened it when Harold bellowed from the other room, “They’ve closed the motorway! Bloody idiots are on the motorway!”
Ethan looked back and cocked an eyebrow. He couldn’t quite believe some of his inebriated family and friends would actually cheer and applaud this.
“I’m sorry we couldn’t stay any longer, mate,” Mike apologised. He stepped into the porch and erected the lapels of his coat.
Ethan shook his head and held up both hands, politely cutting his friend off. “Don’t be stupid. I’m just sorry we didn’t get more of a chance to catch up. Give me a ring when you get home so I know you’re both okay. I hope your mum recovers soon, Emily.”
“Thanks,” she sobbed. “And Happy birthday,”

Ethan smiled and shook Mike’s hand. He then watched the night devour his friends. He waited for them to disappear completely into the inky blackness before locking and bolting the front door.

CHAPTER 4

At nine o'clock the birthday party croaked Death's lonely rattle and drifted into abysmal insignificance. Forty years just wiped off the clock, forgotten about with barbaric regularity. Isaac Newton described time best by saying it was like a "flowing river moving at a constant speed from past to future, never deviating, never looking back, never changing." Ethan Hardcastle didn't know what the next four decades had in store for him (and he didn't want to know), but if there was one hard fact of life he'd learnt today it was this – time waits for nobody.

The disturbances in town had continued over the past couple of hours, increasing in violence. He had encouraged the majority of his guests to return to their homes. Bulletins were broadcast more frequently; shaky, spinning footage recorded on mobile phones, the new camcorder, depicting abandoned streets, looted stores, burning vehicles, and uncontainable rage. Ethan had become hypnotised. In fact, he had found himself watching with fascination as the hooded youths turned the streets of Britain into a kaleidoscope of anarchy.

The bungalow was still haunted with a few stragglers; the hardcore minority who refused to allow a little civil unrest to interfere with their getting steamed. His mother and Harold were still there. They'd called for a taxi – Harold being too pissed to drive – but all they'd got was a busy signal. Ethan's best friend, Bryan Locke, was there, stripping the buffet clean, and Lee Hardcastle seemed happy enough to drink beer and watch the world descend into chaos. It had been a different story an hour ago, though, as he had paced frantically back and forth, burning a hole in the almond carpet, panicking because his wife, an auxiliary nurse working nights, hadn't replied to his tsunami of text messages. Since she'd called back an hour ago and assured him that she was indeed fine, he had kicked back and joined Harold on the sofa to watch the insanity unfold.

Dave Hardcastle – the eldest of the three brothers – had been at home in his apartment when the rioting had begun. He'd called and apologized, told Ethan that unfortunately there was no way he could risk going out in such turmoil. Ethan had agreed with him and, after wishing his youngest sibling a happy birthday, Dave had hung up and not been heard from since.

Ethan slowly opened the bedroom door and crept inside. He winced as the floorboards creaked under his weight. He moved slowly across the room, walking like a man wading through an invisible stream. Ethan crouched beside the single bed and kissed his son on the nose. Five-years-old and owner of an award-winning smile, the bundle of exquisiteness rolled onto his side and groaned a tired little gurgle. Ethan smiled as he watched Lincoln bury his head deeper into the Scooby-Doo pillowcase. He pulled the blue duvet up under his chin and ruffled his sleep-knotted blonde hair gently. Stepping over an assortment of stuffed animals and plastic replicas of Chris Jericho and the red Power Ranger, he stopped in front of the blinded window. The wind howled like a rabid banshee and tested the glass in its frame.

The nightlight in the corner of the room had apparently declared war on the creeping darkness, pumping shades of gentle light into the bedroom, keeping the overbearing blackness at bay. A tremor tumbled down his spine when he realized just how oblique his son's room actually was. His bedroom was at the back of the bungalow, facing the driveway, low, and because the property had been built in such an isolated location by Ethan himself many moons back, there were barely any street lamps. They were only a half hour drive from the trouble in the city, but right then and there, it seemed a universe away. There was a gurgling creek at the back of the house, shrouded in wild shrubbery, and then a huge field opened onto the moors. Ethan usually loved the remoteness of it all; cut off from society by free will, miles from the grime-and-crime of city life. But tonight he didn't like it. Not now it was dark and he was quarantined by acres of nothing, a rioting legion tearing his city apart. Right then and there, he'd have happily traded it all in to be close to a police station.

What the hell's gotten into you? They're hardly going to star rioting outside of your house.

He cranked the dial on the mobile hanging above his son's bed and a lullaby smoothly and softly coaxed Lincoln further into sleep. He leaned over the bed and kissed him on the forehead.

A car alarm went off.

At first Ethan thought it might have been the Pickup in the driveway and his throat constricted, making it hard to swallow. He felt as though a greasy slug was feeding from his oesophagus. Then he realized it was coming from the back of the house, in the distance, far away. He pulled the curtains apart and slipped a finger between the blinds, looking into a pair of wide eyes which belonged to his ghostly reflection. His heart began to pound. And for one awful moment he thought it was going to break free of his rib cage and flop, steaming, onto the bedroom floor.

Bloody hell! What's gotten into you? Car alarms go off around here all the time and you never get spooked. Get a bloody grip, man!
He didn't know what was wrong with him. Ever since the violence had increased, an edgy tension had buzzed through his bowels. His senses were straining to pick up every little noise, every little flutter of movement. Why was he frightened? He was a forty-year-old man. What did he have to be scared of? They were just teenagers breaking into shops to steal trainers. But there was no denying it – he was fucking petrified! It felt as though there was an invisible anvil pressing against his chest, flattening his lungs. The nice little bungalow in the countryside didn't feel so safe tonight. It felt as though Ethan and his family were in the middle of a crumbling society where a nuke was due to explode.

Ethan Hardcastle shook his head at the ridiculousness of it all. These rioters – and that's what they were – were not protesting. They weren't demonstrating. They weren't rallying because Dennison Asaria had died in police custody and they demanded answers. They were doing what they were doing because they wanted to do it. They were using the youth's death as an excuse, sure, but they were lobbing bricks at police, torching vehicles, and looting stores because they knew – as Ethan did – that the British justice system was laughable.

The disorder wasn't race motivated (no matter what the media wanted you to believe) and there wasn't any domineering number of white, black or Asian people involved. There was just a solid mass of stampeding fuckwits hell-bent on causing as much disruption as possible. And what would happen when the police started

to regain control? What punishment would the participants receive – an ASBO?
Ethan crossed the bedroom and quietly opened the door, stepping into the hallway. A barking dog made him pause again. Ethan swallowed hard, feeling as though somebody had dusted his tongue with chalk.
This time the dog wasn't in the distance. It wasn't far away. It was close. It was in his garden. It was his dog!

"Bella," Ethan hissed to himself.

He galloped down the long corridor and barged into the front room just as Karris bellowed, "Ethan! There's somebody in the garden!"

CHAPTER 5

Ethan exploded into the front room, heart beating like a drum, nearly running straight into Bryan Locke in the process and barely avoiding the collision. He held up his hands to apologize and gently shoved him aside.

"What's going on?" he blurted. "Is somebody in the garden?"
"I think so, yeah," Bryan said, leading the other man into the front room. "Lee heard a commotion in the garden. And then your dog started barking."
Ethan glanced at his mother who was sitting on the sofa, enthralled by the ruckus, chewing mechanically at her fingernails. He frowned as he crossed the room and silently hoped things weren't becoming too strained for her. Her health had deteriorated since approaching her late sixties. He smiled, but the gesture felt tight and fake. "Are you okay, Ma?"
"Yes, yes, I'm fine, darling," his mother replied, smiling her own plastic smile. "Lee thought he heard something in your garden, that's all. I told him it was probably just a fox or something. It's nothing to worry about, I'm sure."

Ethan nodded and hoped she was right. "You stay here, okay, Ma? I'm going to check it out."

"Okay, honey. Do be careful."

Ethan stepped in front of the bay window. Bryan was standing beside him like a loyal disciple. Ethan slipped an arm around his wife's thin waist. "Hey, babe, what's wrong?"

"My God, Ethan; Lee thinks he heard something out back," she said, manicured hands clutching the sides of her face Kevin McAllister style. "Then Bella started barking; really barking, barking her head off, she won't stop, you know she only barks at people she doesn't know." When she spoke, the words joined together and crashed into one another like cars in a pileup.

"Okay, okay," Ethan soothed, hoping his calm tone would reassure his blatantly scared wife. "I'll go and check it out. You keep an eye on Mum. Harold, you too, okay? Bryan and I have got this covered." He glanced at his friend, eyes pleading.

"Sure," Bryan said. He moved away from the window and stepped into the kitchen. He slipped a finger between the blinds and looked out, but all he could see was blackness. He swallowed hard; tongue bloated, a strange taste like he had a mouthful of coins making him want to throw up. Ethan stepped up beside him and patted him on a twig-like shoulder. Lee slumped against the wall, slurping from a bottle of beer

"Ethan, you're not going out there!" Karris commanded. Her hands grabbed her husband's top. Her breathing was tight and her face was flushed bright pink. "It's not safe out there, not with all the rioting going on, please don't go outside." Her words were still blending together as though she was emceeing.

"I'll be fine, sweetie," Ethan said. He pecked her on the lips and rubbed the pad of this thumb over her hot cheek. "Besides, I'm not going out there alone. Bryan's coming with me."

"That's right," Bryan snarled. He flexed his bony arms, posing like a wrestler from the 80's. "Everybody knows not to mess with me."

"See? I'll be fine." Ethan smiled. "It's probably nothing."

"But you don't know that for sure."

"No," Ethan sighed. "But I do know for sure that our son is sleeping across the hall. I need to make sure that everything is okay for him."

Karris nodded slowly. The mention of her boy seemed to correct her priorities and allowed her to think clearly. "Okay. You're right. I'm sorry. But take the flashlight with you."

Ethan turned and yanked a drawer open, almost pulling it off the runner in his eagerness. Fingers scrabbled over mobile phone chargers, brochures, takeaway menus, batteries, dog-eared magazines, and then he finally found the rubber-swathed torch. He snatched at it as though it was eternal youth and switched it on, aiming the beam of light onto the kitchen floor. His head was beginning to throb like a rotten tooth in an infected gum.

Ethan opened the door and stepped out into the night. The roaring wind snatched the PVC partition from his grasp and slammed it against the wall, wrenching hinges. It howled into the kitchen and knocked over empty beer cans. Ethan stepped into the darkness and aimed the torch around. The garden was empty. Bright light bounced over the patio table and chairs, exposed the framework of the shed, the wire fence separating his property from the flowing moorlands, before sweeping over the blue, brown, and black recycling bins standing to attention beneath the kitchen window. Nobody was here. And it didn't look like anybody had been either.

The yapping beagle stopped barking as soon as she saw her master. She ran speedily towards Ethan, pink collar jangling. He bent and stroked her brown and white fur,

petting her. "Hey, you're okay, you're okay, girl." He rubbed behind her floppy ears and glanced up at Bryan who merely shrugged his shoulders.
"I guess he was wrong."

Ethan held up a hand to hush his friend. Torchlight danced senselessly. Bryan frowned, then his ears picked up the same thing that Ethan's had. From far away, but probably no more than two miles, came the distant scream of jumbled sirens. Police, ambulances, fire-engines; all gelled together to serenade the smoky night. Their muffled wails were particularly distressing, the distant medley making Ethan want to run inside and lock the door until this crazy night was over.
"Have you heard that?" said Bryan.

Ethan nodded slowly. "Sounds like a thousand sirens going off at the same time."
"More like thousands."

Ethan turned and saw Lee stagger drunkenly into the garden. He had spilled some beer on his Foo Fighters T-shirt. His ears prickled at the strange noise, but his beer-addled brain wasn't sober enough to identify the clamour.
"I heard something, Eth, I'm telling you." He swigged from his bottle again, but missed his mouth.
"There's nothing here now," said Bryan, stating the obvious. "It was probably just the wind."

"It wasn't the wind," said Lee, balancing awkwardly on his heels.
Ethan knew his older brother packed a fiery temper after draining one-too-many. He'd lost count of the number of pointless fights he had started over the years on stag

nights and birthday celebrations and what-not, and he recognized that throaty growl now. His shoulders were up, fists clenched, the posture of an angry man with an itch to scratch.

"I know what I heard, and it wasn't the fucking wind."

"Okay, Lee," Bryan said softly. "You heard it. I didn't."

"Are you calling me a liar?"

"He's not calling you a liar, okay?" Ethan said. He stepped purposefully between the two men, flashlight pointing up, revealing twinkling stars. "Everybody just needs to take a deep breath and relax."

"Ethan!" Karris sailed her voice out of the open back door. "Is everything okay?"

"Everything's fine!" Ethan roared back. He had to strain his voice to make the words audible over the madman cackle of the roaring wind. "Nothing is out here! We're coming back!"

Lee mumbled something low and unintelligible before turning heel and stepping inside the bungalow. Bryan smiled crookedly at Ethan who cocked an eyebrow in response.

"Come on, mate," he said, shaking his head, stepping back into the bright kitchen. He thumbed off the torch and Bryan closed the door behind them.

"There's nothing out there," Ethan confirmed.

"I heard something," Lee quickly added.

"But they've gone now. And that's the most important thing."

The doorbell chimed.

Karris gasped loudly and spun nervously towards the front door. Ethan paused and looked up; eyes wide, heart beating like a jackhammer, blood tingling in his arteries. For the first time that evening, Harold Singleton put his can of Guinness down and looked away from the TV. Bryan and Lee – apparently no longer enemies – wandered out of the kitchen and glanced at the builder.

"What's this about now?" Lee slurred.

"It's okay," Ethan said. "I'll get it."

"Who is it?" Karris stupidly asked.

"I kind of need to open the door first, babe," Ethan answered with a smile.

He strolled purposefully down the hallway, striding with gait, furious that somebody should have the stones to ring his doorbell whilst his son was asleep.

It's probably one of the guests from earlier, too bloody pissed to remember their phone or their house keys or something. Bloody morons!

Fingers encircled the latch and pulled the front door open, about to unleash one hell of a tongue-thrashing on the arsehole on the other side, but his breath lodged in his throat when nothing but the yowling wind greeted him. He stepped onto the porch, arms folded, face moody, eyes searching the shadows like a sniper choosing his next victim. There was nobody there. The sirens were a fraction louder now he was at the front of the house and he stepped zealously into his work boots without bothering to lace them up. Ethan sighed wearily as he crunched his way across the driveway.

The Pickup was still parked in the same position as earlier, untouched, the stack of timber still waiting to be stored in the garage. And he ran curious eyes over his brother's and Harold's cars, but they too were fine. Ethan stepped back inside, shaking his head, muttering something about "pesky kids" when three noises - dum-dum-dum - came from the front room, quickly followed by the screaming of his wife and mother.

CHAPTER 6

"Eggs," Bryan said, pointing torchlight over the window and revealing the smeared pane. It looked as though somebody with a bad chest-cold had spewed phlegm all over it. He glanced over at Ethan who was standing behind him, searching for the bastards responsible. Bella was still running ecstatically at his heels.
"Little fuckers," Ethan hissed.

"Why would somebody egg your house?"

"I don't know," said Ethan. He disappeared beneath thick shrubbery at the bottom of the garden, cursing loudly when he almost tripped over the yapping dog. "Somebody must want to play silly buggers."

Karris stepped into the doorway, arms folded over heaving chest, a blanket shielding her from the callous wind. She looked tired and frightened. She'd scraped her hair back into a ponytail and her cheeks were flushed. "You see anything, baby?" The need for the pet name at that moment was as necessary as her next breath. It reassured her; banished her fears. But then the wind gobbled up the words and mimicked her safety.
"No," Ethan said. Ambling through knee-high grass, he rubbed his grubby hands on his jeans. "Whoever it was has gone."
"Do you think it was the same person who rang the doorbell?" Karris asked. She spoke in a jittery tone, as though she was expecting it to ring again at any moment. The air reeked of oily smoke. Sirens seemed a little quieter.

"Probably just kids messing about," Ethan said. He placed the torch on the glass surface of the patio table. "They've gone now."
He turned and gave the moors a lingering glance.

Karris raised an eyebrow. "All the way up here?"

Ethan shrugged his shoulders. "I don't know, Karris; what else could it be?"
"Good Lord," Ethan's mother's voice peppered the night. "I don't believe it."
Ethan stepped back inside the bungalow. Overhead fluorescents assaulted his eyes, rendering him sightless for a few seconds, and he blinked rapidly to regain composure before walking through to the front room. Harold and Lee were standing in front of the TV, both talking loudly, both nursing beers. His mother was quietly sobbing into a crumpled paper handkerchief. Harold looked over to her and frowned before taking another gulp of Guinness and turning back to the TV. Ethan's blood boiled. Right then and there he could have ripped Harold Singleton's head from his scrawny shoulders. Right then and there he could have killed the man.
Ethan crossed to his mother and crouched down beside her, taking her hand in his and kissing the back of it. "Hey, hey," he comforted, "it's alright, Ma, it's going to be just fine." He pulled her towards him, cradling her exactly the same way she used to cradle him as a child suffering a particularly horrible nightmare. "There's nothing to be frightened of. I'm here. It's just kids. They've gone now. I'm sure they won't come back."

His mother shook her head and tried to control her sobbing. "No, honey, you don't understand." When she spoke the words were muffled due to the handkerchief she was speaking into. “The news,” she sobbed, fresh tears rolling down her cheeks and leaving trails of mascara. “They’ve just found the body of a poor policeman. He’d been stabbed thirty-three times in the chest and face.” She paused and swallowed rising bile.

Ethan glanced across to the TV and saw a reporter standing in front of yellow POLICE: DO NOT CROSS tape. Forensic officers wearing full-bodied blue coveralls moved slowly about the cordoned area. Ethan frowned and stood up, his brain not wanting to believe what his eye and ears were faxing across. The young reporter spoke hurriedly, as though he couldn’t wait to get the job done and dash back to the safety of the studio.

“The body of Officer Ellison was found by riot police with an appallingly large number of stab wounds,” the reporter said, looking fretfully into the camera. “Immediately the area behind me was cleared of previously free-roaming looters who eyewitnesses have described as “savages”. The Prime Minister is due to make a statement at any moment condemning the needless death of Officer Ellison as well as the barbarous behaviour here in Manchester.”

Ethan sprung up like a fully cranked Jack-in-the-box. His eyes narrowed. “What? Manchester? What the hell does he mean?” He directed the question towards his brother.

Lee leered drunkenly.

Does he actually find some perverted humour in all of this?

Ethan swallowed hard and heard something click in his throat.

"The rioting has spread," Lee said, shrugging his shoulders. "They're rioting in Nottingham, Birmingham, Manchester, Liverpool—"
"They have really torn up Liverpool," Harold quickly interjected.
"Apparently there's been about twelve quid worth of damage."
Both men laughed hysterically.

Ethan opened his mouth to say something when the sound of Karris yapping like a trapped puppy made him look up. Bella was barking over excitedly again. There was a brief commotion in the garden. Pottery smashed. Something fell over. Footsteps scampered across the patio. And then both Karris and Bryan were calling his name frantically. He bounced through the kitchen like a human pinball and ran out into the cold night, searching for the source that had spooked his wife and best mate so badly.
The youth was standing cockily at the bottom of the garden, behind the wire fence, standing on the moors, hard to see at first. In fact, if he hadn't been smoking a cigarette then he would have probably gone unnoticed altogether. He was a black blip on blank radar...but he was there.

Ethan glanced over to his wife who was shrieking unintelligibly into her cupped hands. He shoved past her and focused on the small orange spot piercing the shrouding darkness. Then the unmistakable aroma of burning marijuana flitted past his nostrils and Ethan Hardcastle finally saw the youth standing amongst the stinging nettles and brambles properly. His hood was up and, unless he was mistaken, one hand was stuffed down the front of his ridiculously baggy trousers.
"Karris," Ethan whispered, "go inside."

The youth took another drag from the joint and lolled his head back, looking as though he was growing impatient.

"What does he want?"

"Go and check on Lincoln."

"But what does he want?"

"Will you just fucking do as I ask?" Ethan snarled, spittle flying.
Karris nodded and obediently went back inside.

Ethan took a step forward.

Bryan reliably followed.

"Hey there," Ethan called. His voice teemed with friendliness. He was aware that he sounded like a rep conversing with a tourist. "Are you lost or something, mate? It's a bad night to be out on the moors."

No response.

Ethan took another cautious step forward.

Lacy fingers pulled the full moon out of a wedge of thick cloud and in its revealing glow Ethan could see the youngster more clearly. A scarf was wrapped around his nose and mouth, the hood of his jacket concealing the top half of his face. A jungle of jewellery hung around his neck. Ethan could only estimate his age. There really was that little to work with. Judging by his bright red tracksuit and mansion-sized trainers, Ethan figured he was around eighteen or nineteen. He was certainly no older.

Ethan nodded to nobody in particular and took one final step forward. He was now standing in front of the wire fence.
"How old's the dog, mate?"

Ethan looked down at the barking beagle. His heart was pounding hard. He could hear it throbbing in his ears. Passively, he raised his hands, palms outward.
"She's only seven months old. She's just a puppy."

The youth laughed loudly, gloved hands clutching his stomach like he'd just learned he'd won the lottery.

"Nah, bro, you're not gettin' me," he chuckled. He sucked from the joint once more. Ash flicked deliberately through the fence. "I mean your girl."
"What? What did you say?"

"The bitch," the youth sneered. "How old's the bitch, mate?"
Ethan gripped the wire fence with talons of hatred. "Say that again, dickhead! Come on! I dare you! I fucking dare you!" Fingers rolled into fists. His arm drew back into a sling-shot position.
The youth laughed again and a plume of wet-earth reeking smoke billowed into Ethan's face. "Chill, chill; you're goin' to flat-line a blood vessel or some shit." Despite the whiteness around his eyes, Ethan could have been forgiven for thinking he was speaking to a hoodlum straight out of LA or Detroit. "I'm just fuckin' with you, pops. Don't go havin' no heart attack or anythin', yeah?"

"Are you the little bastard that egged my house?" Ethan snarled. He squared up to the fence, chest puffed like a proud pigeon. "Been playing silly beggars, eh? Think you're a big man? I've got a little boy in there." He pointed over his shoulder with a crooked thumb. "And your shenanigans better not have woken him up, o—"

"Or what? What're you goin' do about it?" His voice cranked with bass, but lost most of its gangster twang. Arms flailed into the air, making him look like the Christ the Redeemer statue on a dark windy night in Brazil.

Ethan instinctively flinched and regretted it immediately.

"Yeah, we threw eggs at your house! So fuckin' what? You ain't goin' to do anythin' about it! Drivin' about tonight, we hear the news! It's bedlam out there. No police anywhere. Y'all could rob Fort Knox and get away with it!"
He said we! He said we threw eggs! He said driving about tonight we hear the news! There's more than just him!

Time to inject a note of rile into his voice. "Well, listen to me, sonny," Ethan wagged his finger, but icicles were playing volleyball with his heart. "You chose the wrong bloody house to—"

"Nah, mate, you chose the wrong house!" The words tumbled from his mouth like rockery on a precarious ledge. "All the way out here; away from the city, away from the police, no neighbours. And on a night like tonight, too; riotin' in the city, all police removed from the streets, nobody allowed in, nobody allowed out." He shook his hooded head as though he had genuine sympathy for Ethan's predicament. "What the hell were you thinkin' movin' your family out here?"

CHAPTER 7

Lincoln was awake. Something – be it the fanatical wind or his father's raised voice – had disturbed him and now he was bawling blue murder. Karris galloped down the corridor and barged into his bedroom, her burdensome heart still throbbing from the confrontation with the stranger in the garden. Lincoln was out of bed, red-faced, standing in the centre of the room, disorientated, screaming out his tiny lungs, stomping bare feet. Karris picked up her crying son and pressed his head against her shoulder, crossing the bedroom.

As far as she knew, Ethan and Bryan were still outside, but she didn't have a clue what was happening. And she didn't think she wanted to know.
What did he want? Where had he come from? Who was he with?
The questions zoomed around her brain, pestering as they burned rubber, convincing her that the stranger's arrival was more than just inadvertent – it was ominous! The moorlands (or Peak View as it was more commonly known) weren't just some magical speckle of fairy dust waiting to be slap-banged on a postcard and cooed over. Yes, it was beautiful, but it also had a perilously brutal side which could hurt, maim, and yes, even kill on such a barbaric and fucked-up night. Some of the cliffs in the area plunged 300 feet down to a rocky bottom. And although bears and boars weren't known to wander freely through the English countryside, unseen deer darting in front of two bulleting headlights on a rainy night could, and had, the potential to turn lethal. You didn't have to be crazy to be on the moors on such an eccentric night – you had to be fucking suicidal! "Mummy," Lincoln sobbed.

"Hey, honey-bear,"

"I feel sick, Mummy."
"You do?"

Lincoln nodded his head and rubbed his eyes.

"Let's go get you a glass of water then."

She scooped up her world and was just about to leave the room when she heard a noise that made her breath catch in her throat and suffocate her. A faded crash followed by a somewhat faded whump and suddenly the drums in her ears were pinging and tentacles of bright light were invading the room.
What the hell was that?

She ambled across the cluttered bedroom and pulled the curtains apart, separating the blinds, breathing rashly, looking beyond her own ghostlike reflection, and what she saw made her want to disappear down the Yellow Brick Road and conceal herself in the Emerald City forever.

When she had been a teenager – fourteen or fifteen – this bitch of a school bully called Hayley Osborne had made her life a living hell. Karris had been plump as a child; not overweight, not exactly slim either, but that hadn't stopped this tramp from lifting Karris's jumper and shouting things like "Hey, she's got a pillow up her top, oh no, wait, it's just her fat belly!"
Of course, kids being kids (nasty little shitty brats with more gob than consideration), it didn't take long before she was constantly being labelled fat and made fun of. Her few close friends quickly became either embarrassed or afraid of hanging out with her, and she eventually

suffered, as no child, should with depression. The happy social butterfly bloomed into a loathsome tomboyish loner who despised even her own appearance, snapped at people easily, often losing her temper, crying for no reason, then becoming majorly overactive, rarely sleeping. Then the self-harming had begun.

Even though Hayley and her cowardly cronies had never actually harmed a hair on her head, Karris grew to hate school with a passion. The panic attacks rattled her. Everything else she could cope with; that constant current of nervousness churning inside her stomach, diarrhoea, the shortness of breath, the choking sensation, the chest pain, vomiting, heart palpitations, but those panic attacks had almost been too much. In fact, if her father hadn't come home from work one morning with the world's biggest migraine and found her in the cellar with his cut-throat razor, she shuddered to think what could have happened.

That was why when she looked through the bedroom window and saw five terrible incarnations of Hayley circling Harold's burning Ford, her bowels liquefied and her mouth became parched. She watched in a paralysed stupor as they cheered and jeered as the petrol bomb really began to incinerate the vehicle. They were all silhouetted by the brightness of the crackling flames, but from the bedroom window she could see they were all wearing hoods with either a scarf or a bandanna covering the lower halves of their faces, concealing their identities, protecting against the choking fumes. Karris could feel the scream buzzing in her lungs, but for the first time in seven years that same blockage that had prevented her from telling her parents about Hayley had suddenly reappeared, and she couldn't form the words. She tried. She really tried. But the fear had already settled into the neighbourhood.

One cocky youth swaggered too close to the burning car and something underneath exploded, flinging the yob onto the grass verge at the side of the house. The ear-splitting eruption thankfully alerted the others.

Another youth stepped in front of the window. His baseball cap was pulled low and the collar of his T-shirt stood to attention. He didn't have a bandanna around his face or a scarf, and when he obnoxiously strolled past, alpha maleness oozing from his pores, he stopped dead and looked at Karris. The flickering flames flashed an arrogant smile. A gloved hand slapped against the window, startling her, making her leap from her skin quicker than any school tyrant ever could. Laughter bellowed into the room. Ready for how ruthless and aggressive they were?

Harold suddenly appeared at the front door and swayed unsteadily into the rectangle of light spilling from the open doorway. He saw the fiery wreck which had once been his beloved Ford, crappy though it was, and he started shouting and pointing and threatening and cursing. The flock of teenagers backed away, laughing at this old relic, but aware that he possessed something of a threat. Now Belinda Hardcastle, Ethan's mother, was in the doorway. Her mobile was pressed to the side of her face, no doubt calling the police and the fire brigade. Harold turned back to the house, red-faced, breathing like he had just completed a marathon, and barked something about staying away from the fire to Belinda. He'd just made it back to the front door, hands on his hips, when one of the little villains separated themselves from the brooding pack and ran forward, throwing something black and square high into the air. The makeshift mortar rotated once before hitting Harold on the back of the head. He dropped like a ton of bricks – not just one – and lost consciousness immediately. Blood dribbled at first and then began pumping steadily from the jagged wound at the back of his skull, pooling underneath, spreading out. Belinda stepped outside, screaming, the phone dropping to the floor, and Karris's eyes widened with horror when another youth ran down the driveway and kicked Harold in the head.

"OH JESUS CHRIST!" Belinda bellowed into the dark night. "HELP ME! SOMEBODY HELP ME!"

They had already knocked him out with a brick, but that didn't stop them from circling his limp body and kicking him in the ribs, booting him in the head, stomping on his groin, the whole time hurtling a barrage of abuse at Belinda. A silhouette stepped in front of Belinda, arms outstretched as though two invisible claimants were tugging in opposite directions, and the wind blew the hood free.

Oh my God! It's a girl!

Karris Hardcastle, still rooted to the spot by fear, refused to believe what her eyes were displaying. How could society have been allowed to crumble to such a degrading depth? When she had been a little girl such things as drug abuse, violence, teenage delinquency, family meltdowns, benefits, binge drinking, children that killed, teenage pregnancies, were all completely unheard of. In fact, if either her or her sister had disrespected their parents and spoke to them the same way that some kids spoke nowadays, she probably would have never lived long enough to have had a caesarean. Blood began to boil like water in a kettle as she watched this teenage monster – no more than fourteen years old – spit in Belinda's face and call her "a useless bitch!"

Lee finally barged from the house and began swinging his arms as though he was in a boxing ring with Mike Tyson, fists finding their mark, a conveyor belt of threats spewing from his mouth. He grabbed a handful of the girl's coat and shoved her onto her skinny backside. Then he pushed his mother back towards the house. One hooded youth jumped forward and crunched Lee's jaw, stunning him, knocking him to the ground between a burning wreck and his defenceless mother. Another pushed through the crowd and kicked him twice in the spine.

That's it! You've seen enough! What're you going to do – just stand here and watch your family get murdered?

Karris pushed herself away from the window and ran out of the room, sprinting like a greyhound chasing a mechanical rabbit down the corridor. Ethan and Bryan had just stepped inside the kitchen, her husband blatantly pissed about something, and they stepped back to avoid clashing.

"Ethan! Thank God!"

The builder closed the back door and locked it. He bent over and penetrated the wall with the deadbolt. Bryan turned towards Karris and raised his eyebrows.

"What the hell was that noise? It sounded like an explosion."

"It was," Karris panted. "They're around the front of the house. They've attacked Harold and Lee." She handed Lincoln over to his father.

"What?" Ethan crossed into the front room and picked up his mobile phone from the sideboard.

Battery's bloody dead!

Cursing, he snatched up the receiver of the house phone and dialled the police. There was a brief click of open air before an automated voice told him: "You have reached the emergency services, but, regrettably, due to the widespread rioting, all police officers have been dispatched and no further units are currently available. If your call is in connection with a life or death incident then please hold the line and we will attempt to answer your call." "Shit," Ethan hissed through a wall of tightly clenched pearls. He slammed the receiver down, kissed his son on one hot cheek, and then handed him back to his wife. Bryan pushed past and ran out of the front door.
"Are the police on their way?" Karris asked. She was hopeful despite the fact that she already knew the answer. He hadn't even spoken to anyone.
"No," Ethan said. "The police aren't available. They're too busy dealing with the bloody rioting in town. This is what happens when the government cut back on police!"

"Ethan, wait," Karris said, grabbing him by the elbow and pulling him gently back. "There's something you need to know."
"What is it, Karris?"

"They've hurt Harold."

"Little bastards,"

"No, you don't understand. They've really hurt him. They hit him around the head with something. I think it might have been a brick."
Ethan Hardcastle inhaled hard.
"I think he may be dead."

"I'm sure he'll be okay. I'll check on him. Are they still out there?"
"They were."

"Okay. There was one in the back garden, too."

"What happened?"

"Nothing, he was just trying to intimidate me."

"Saying what?"

"It's not important. He's gone now. Look, stay here and keep trying to get through to the police."

Karris rushed obediently across the lounge and snatched the house phone from the cradle. Before she could even dial the number another explosion, this one much more powerful than its predecessor, shook the very foundations of the bungalow. A plume of black smoke washed inside the house. Lincoln intensified his caterwauling.
"Stay here!" Ethan commanded, spiralling around the L-shaped sofa. "I'll be right back." He ran out of the house and slipped quietly into the smoky night, taking stock of the horrendous sight. Karris was right – Harold was down and out, blood spilling from his head. His mother - his sixty-eight-year-old mother - was scrapping with a girl five decades younger than her. The teenage bitch was slap-slap-slapping his mother's head, scratching false nails down the sides of her face, trying to drag her to the ground. His mother, admittedly no battleaxe, was holding her own though. Handfuls of hair were torn from the girl's Croydon facelift, and her emaciated skeleton was no match for his mother's stout body.

Two of the vicious bastards were really laying into Lee, but somehow his older brother was managing to fight back. That Tabasco-temper of his was being splashed everywhere, spicing things up, punches merely fanning flames, and Ethan, frozen to the spot, watched as he snatched a length of wood from the back of the Pickup and began swinging as though he was Joaquin Phoenix on a baseball field.

Ethan stepped forward, feeling as though he was taking his first ginger steps on another planet, and before he could become entangled with the nearest youth, Lee's Honda exploded, catching Ethan off guard, and the ground rushed up to smack him in the face.

CHAPTER 8

His brain began to stir and, slowly, his eyes quivered open. Something resembling a confused groan spilled from his cracked lips and when he finally craned his head from the floor a couple of inches, the world began to spin as though his head was attached to a bungee cord. Left side of his face was painfully numb, felt raw, tight, like the time he'd fallen asleep on a sun lounger in Santorini and the sun had charbroiled one side of his face. He'd looked a right twat for the next three days of that holiday. The other side of his face seemed bizarrely bloated, the top of his neck and under his jaw tender, as though he had groomed with a ten year old razor. Flat on his back, knees arched, arms flapped out like a snow-angel that had just been mistaken for a clay pigeon. His ears were ringing. His eyes were watering. Ethan Hardcastle rolled onto his side, wincing as tiny daggers of gravel pinned into his arms and hands. He looked up at the burning cacophony his driveway had become.

Tongues of orange and yellow and red flame leapt dangerously close, aberrant tendrils of blistering flare reaching out for him, dancing manically into the pitch black night. Enormous plumes of petrol-reeking smoke spewed everywhere. Ethan retched. The vile stench made him want to cough up his scorched lungs. Unsteadily, he climbed to his knees and held one charred arm up, the only pitiful defence he had to such searing heat. It felt as though somebody had locked him inside an incinerator and turned the bastard on.

Harold's crappy Ford and Lee's Honda were both ablaze. Flames and toxic fumes spewed from the ruptured fuel tanks, climbing illicitly into the dark night. Ethan narrowed his eyes and observed the two burning metallic skeletons through a wave of nausea.

Even the tyres are on fire!

It looked as though one of the vehicles had been set alight by the youths and the fiery aftermath had torched the neighbouring car, too. For some reason, he glanced over at the Pickup and released a sigh of relief when he saw the beast still parked there, untouched, on the opposite side of the driveway.
Suddenly Bryan was in front of him.

Grabbing Ethan by the elbow, he pointed at the two burning wrecks, jabbering ecstatically about something. Ethan couldn't hear what. The ringing in his ears had made him a deaf man, the horrendous sight in the driveway rendering him speechless. Ethan reached out and grabbed his friend with trembling fingers, steadying himself, propping himself up against him. Bryan's nose was bleeding. He had a nasty-looking gash on his lower lip, too.
"What...what the...hell..." Ethan couldn't finish the sentence. An elevator of bile was rising up his gullet. Instead, he clutched his heart and threw up in the gutter.
"We need to get back inside!" Bryan screamed, grabbing the builder by the hips, swinging him around. "We need to get back inside right now!" Bellowing filled the narrow canals of his ears, yet still the raucous screech of creaking, twisting metal dwarfed it. Glazed eyes peered into his best mate's face, and it was clear nothing was registering.

"Karris and Lincoln are safe. They are inside the house," Bryan pointlessly continued, rubbing the back of his hand over his sweaty forehead. "We need to get to your mum, though."

Ethan was still staring into the flickering bonfire, strands of puke dangling from his chin. Bryan stepped in front of the man, aware that his hearing had been battered, and pointed towards the front door of the bungalow.
The Devil's steaming cold hand gripped his heart and squeezed.
His mother was kneeling in the driveway; sobbing uncontrollably, cradling Harold's head in her lap, stroking blood-spattered hair, promising the obviously dead corpse that everything was going to be okay. Behind her, Lee was breaking his heart into his sleeve, a length of timber still in his white-knuckled grip. Ethan lurched forward and almost tumbled into the ferocious melee. The disgusting stench of boiled petrol drifted through the air like incense.

"Mum!" Ethan howled, staggering drunkenly on legs that no longer felt capable of supporting him. He slipped once but refused to go down, instead allowing gravity to take over and determine his descent. He landed with a numb thud beside his mother. "Are you okay, Ma?" Ethan shouted, scrambling to his knees and wrapping her up in his thick arms. She was still clutching Harold's dead body, howling, wailing, blood-caked fingers stroking his blood-smeared hair. Now that Ethan was crouching beside the corpse, he could see that the back of the man's skull had been caved in like a rotten pumpkin. His stomach began to contract. "We need to get back inside the house."

"How could they do this? How could they hurt my poor Harold?"
Ethan breathed in sharply.

"I don't know."

"You don't know?"

"Look, Ma, we need to get back inside. They could come back at any moment."
"I know...I keep...trying...to wake Harold...but..."

Bryan jogged between mother and son and stepped beside Lee, looking like two medieval sentinels protecting their kingdom. Lee did, in fact, brandish the length of wood as though it were a samurai sword. He had stopped crying now, and for that Ethan was grateful. Right now he didn't have time to console his mother, never mind his brother. Getting back inside the bungalow was his only priority.

"Ma, listen to me—"

"Harold? Harold, darling, it's time to wake up. It's not safe out here."
"He can't hear you, Ma."

"What are you talking about?"

"You know what I'm talking about."

Karris was suddenly in the doorway behind him, a screaming, wriggling Lincoln pressed to her chest. She poked her head into the calamity and searched for her husband.

"Ethan? Ethan? Oh, thank God you're okay."

He looked across to Lee.

"Get Ma inside,"

“I can’t believe this is happening.”

“Lee, we don’t have time for this right now. We need to get back inside and call the police. They could come back at any second.”

“I hope the little sons of bitches do,” Lee snarled. Fingers tightened around his makeshift weapon. Eyes constantly scanned the smoky shadows for movement. “I hope they all come back. I’ll happily do time for each of the little bastards.”

“Hey, what say we stop all of this macho bullshit, eh?”

Karris dipped onto the patio with the same brown blanket she had swathed herself with no more than half an hour ago. Had only thirty minutes passed? It felt more like an eternity! She draped it over her mother-in-law’s buckled shoulders and crouched beside her. “Hey, Belinda, are you okay?”

Ethan impatiently stepped forward, but she ushered him away with her hand. Something on one of the cars exploded and shook the gravel beneath his feet.

“Look, I know Harold has been...hurt,” she chose the words carefully, her face mere inches from the other woman’s, “but your grandson is really frightened. He doesn’t know what’s happening. And he really needs a big cuddle off his grandma, okay? Can you do that?”

Red-rimmed eyes stared at Karris. Trembling lips opened, but the words were as stubborn as a mule. Karris grabbed a hold of her hand and silently shuddered. It was like holding a chunk of ice.

“Come on,” she said, using her son to entice the older woman inside. “Give me a hand settling Lincoln. Ethan and Lee will take care of Harold, right?”

"Sure. I'll look after him, okay, Ma?"

"I...need to...well...okay..." his mother mumbled, stepping over the threshold and taking one last lingering look at her dead lover. Fresh tears began to well up in her eyes and Ethan was positive he could hear his heart crack.

"Do take care of him," she blubbered. "He means so...much..."
She couldn't finish the sentence. She was crying uncontrollably again. This time it did more than just sadden Ethan, it terrified him. It was the timorous sobbing of a woman whose heart and lungs refused to operate without her beloved partner.
Then, with Karris supporting from one side and Bryan holding her up on the other, they stepped back inside the dark house.
Ethan waited for a second until he was certain they'd gone and then looked over to his brother.

"What the hell are we going to do?"

"I don't know."

Ethan yanked his paint-flecked work phone out of his jeans, thumbed the nine button three times and jammed the old Nokia between his shoulder and jaw. The same automated voice informed him that "...due to the widespread rioting all police officers have been dispatched and no further units are available..."
"Even if we could get through, the police are too busy dealing with the rioters to respond."

Lee balled his fist and punched it into the wall in frustration.

“This is crazy.”

“I know.”

“What happened?” Ethan wanted to know. He walked quickly over to his Pickup and pulled a crumpled sheet of blue tarpaulin free. He untied it and returned to the corpse, dragging the plastic sheet behind him. “The explosion knocked me spark out.”
“I’m not sure,” Lee replied. He grabbed an end and blanketed Harold’s body. “I didn’t really see. They petrol-bombed Harold’s car first and then mine exploded, too. I think the heat made it blow. I was trying to put it out when I heard shouting. They must have kicked him to death.”

Ethan nodded and swallowed hard. Then he lowered the tarpaulin over Harold’s corpse as though it were a duvet of reanimation.

CHAPTER 9

Hallway:

Sitting on cord carpet; hands covering face, back leaning against the wall, breathing raspy, Ethan Hardcastle had a few seconds to take stock of events. His home was under attack; driveway had become a flaring combustion of fire, future stepfather had been murdered by a cloudburst of stomping feet, mother was inconsolable, brother was tirelessly promising all kinds of vengeful retribution, head throbbing due to being knocked unconscious, Lincoln petrified, best friend a silent shadow of his former self.

Ethan pulled his knees into his stomach and sank his teeth into his knuckles. He could hear his mother sobbing in the kitchen now; could hear Karris pointlessly trying to comfort her; could hear Lincoln screaming, vomiting up his lungs, but he, his father, didn't move. He couldn't move! He tried to put up a fight, but it was useless. How was he supposed to wrestle with his feelings when Harold's blood still stained his hands? His arms were just too short to box with his emotions. With a choked sob he began to cry for a stepfather he barely knew and a biological father he'd barely met.

CHAPTER 10

"So what do we do now?"

Bryan Locke stopped dead centre in the middle of the smoky kitchen and flung his phone onto the draining board. It landed with a hollow clang. He had just tried ringing his mother, but all he'd received was the same busy signal. Then he'd anxiously began scrolling through his phonebook, starting with his ex-wife, finishing with his lawyer, but each time the line had been unaccountably jammed.

He turned, directing the question individually to the people seated around the table. His face was flushed and streaked with greasy soot. Having been punched in the nose during the skirmish, blood had dried between nostrils and upper lip, looking like spilled petrol on the Atacama floor.

"Call the police," Belinda said. Nervously, she continued to tear the paper tissue apart. "We need to get them up here now."

"That's not going to happen, Ma," Ethan said for what must have been the hundredth time. "The lines are down. I've already told you this."

"Who were they? That's what I want to know," Lee said. The wood slapped into the palm of his free hand.

"I don't know."

"They must have chosen this place for a reason."

"Like what, Lee?"

"You tell me."

"I'm hardly smuggling cocaine in the cellar."

"Don't be stupid. That's not what I meant."

"Then what did you mean?"

"Something must have made them choose tonight. That's all I'm saying."
"Yeah," Ethan growled, blood pressure rising. "The fact that the little bastards knew they could get away with it."

"Who they were isn't important. Where they are now is," Bryan said. He fretfully glanced through the window, eyes blurry, vision misty. He was beginning to stink like a fireman who had just extinguished a blaze in a smokehouse. "They could be watching the house right now."
"Don't say that," Karris said. She had expertly rocked Lincoln into a relatively peaceful sleep. He was now sprawled on the sofa in the living room. The door was open so they could keep a worried eye on him.

"I didn't mean to frighten you."
"Too late for that,"

"I doubt they'll come back, sweetheart," Ethan said, crossing to the sink and turning the faucet on. He winced as cold water quenched his blistered throat.
"How do you know that for sure?" Lee asked.

"I don't," Ethan admitted, wiping his mouth on the back of his hand. "But they were kids, that all I'm saying."

“What?” Lee screamed through a whisper. “They kick Harold to death. They torch two fucking cars, and you say they were just kids?”

“Keep your voice down,” Ethan warned. He stood up and peeped through the window, fearing what he would see, before turning around. Their features were distorted due to the cloud of smoke hanging over the table. It looked as though somebody had judged a bonfire competition in his garden and forgot to inform him. “Okay then, what we have here is Hobson’s choice. The police aren’t going to show up and obviously it’s not safe here. My Pickup’s parked right outside. I say we get in it and drive into the city.”

“Where they’re rioting?” Lee mumbled.

“Have you got a better idea?”

“It’s crazy! I say we hunt the little bastard’s down. Exact a little revenge.”

“That’s fantastic! Now tell me, have you got anything that doesn’t involve my five-year-old son remaking Death Wish, eh? Have you got anything like that?”

“Well, let’s go with your idea. Say we make it into the city. What then?”

“We make it to Dave’s flat. Maybe we’ll have better luck contacting the police from there.”

“But we can’t all fit in your truck, honey,” Karris pointed out, seizing an interlude between the quarrelling brothers to try to reclaim the peace. The last thing they needed right now was to turn on each other.

“No, you’re right. But we could empty the lumber out of the back. Everybody could fit in there. Look, I know it’s not ideal, but we could try and make—”

“What about Harold?” his mother politely interrupted.

Ethan paused underneath the archway, fingers already clutching the keys to his Pickup. He looked down at the floor and silently wished it would open and gobble him up.

“What about him?”

“Do we take him with us?”

“He’s dead, Ma.”

“So?”

“I don’t think it matters where we leave him.”

“So we just dump him here?”

“No, that’s not what I said.”

“But it’s what you’re saying.”

What? Wait a minute, when did I become the bad guy?

He could sense an argument brewing now, not only with his older brother but also his mother too. He was desperate to dodge both bullets. He wasn’t the wrongdoer here. There just wasn’t enough juice in his reserves to face a confrontation. Tell-tale signs contemporaneously bubbled in front of his eyes though; brooding shoulders, wide eyes, flustered cheeks.

“Look, just listen to me for a second—”

"You never did like Harold, did you?"

"What?"

"Never gave him a fair chance."

"That's ridiculous! I barely knew him, Ma."

"Didn't stop you from looking down your nose at him though, did it?"

"Are you serious?" Ethan laughed humourlessly. He could not believe he was being dragged unwillingly into this argument.

This is insane! There are fucking yobs attacking my house and all she wants to do is probe me about my relationship with Harry! Fucking madness!

"Belinda, love, I don't think now is the right time to be discussing this," Karris said, defending her husband's honour but also remaining calm. "We're all a little scared right now. Everybody just needs to take a deep breath and relax."

"No offense, love," Belinda batted back, "but this hasn't got anything to do with you." She scraped her chair back and stood up. Flickering flames from outside painted her in lucid shades of red and orange.

"What's wrong with you, Ma?" Ethan challenged. "Why would you say such a thing? I know you're upset, I am too, but—" "You? Upset? Don't make me laugh!" Belinda pointed a finger at her youngest son, mock laughter emitting from her. Her head cocked back as she sold the artificialness to the highest bidder. Ethan was suddenly transported thirty years into the past, being scolded for spilling a drink on the brand new sofa. "You could never tolerate Harold."

“That’s not true.”

“You always thought he was going to replace that pitiable excuse of a father of yours, didn’t you?”

“Ma, please—”

“I bet you’re even glad he’s dead!”

“That’s enough!” Karris shouted.

“Shut your mouth!” Belinda screamed back with so much vehemence it left tiny scars on her soul. “I’ve told you once already! This hasn’t got anything to do with you! I won’t tell you again!”

Little stars of light danced erotically in front of his eyes and a sharp, stinging sensation burned his already swollen left cheek. It took a few seconds and then it suddenly dawned on him – his sixty-eight-year-old mother had just slapped him. He hadn’t been struck since childhood. Before he could recover, his mother unleashed a downpour of violence on him, open-palmed slaps reddening cheeks, tiny fists pounding the sides of his skull, fingernails scratching his throat and neck.
“This is your fault,” his mother bellowed. “It shouldn’t be Harold lying dead out there, it should be you! You should be the one who died!”
Her assault was beginning to lose much of its pugnacity and even though her frail fists were still bouncing off his broad chest, Ethan managed to envelop her in his thick arms and, despite her timorous resistance, he pulled her towards him, embracing her. She was sobbing now, heartbreakingly sobbing. He held her like this for a long time. Ten minutes later and it was decided who would be

staying and who would be going. Fifteen minutes later and Ethan and Karris and Lincoln were driving towards a combustible city.

CHAPTER 11

Check this out: eleven o'clock, chucking out time, one hour before the birth of a new day, but as the Pickup was steered along the crowded high street; Ethan Hardcastle could have been forgiven for thinking the circus was performing during an eclipse. There were hundreds – thousands – of feral youngsters on the packed street. Some of them looked no older than ten or eleven years of age.

Jesus Christ! The news got it right. They were telling the truth for once! They weren't scaremongering, they've really taken over!
Curls of smoke drifted from halfway up a looming tower block.
Has someone started a fire in that skyscraper? Surely not!

Nobody was rushing to evacuate the building and, drawing nearer, he could see a crowd gathered beneath, celebrating, cheering, drinking beer. His side window was rolled all the way up but as he crawled past he could hear them singing, "We don't need no water – let the motherfucker burn!" Ethan craned his neck to check on Lincoln, who was strapped in the back. He wasn't happy. The bizarre circumstances had left him bewildered and exhausted. God alone knew what he must be thinking. He traded nervous glances with Karris when they saw an ambulance tipped over like a discarded toy amongst the bedlam.
"My God," Karris mumbled. Her breath misted the windscreen. "We should have stayed at home."

"We had no choice."

"But look at it!"

"They killed Harold!"

"I know. But do you really think anybody here will help?"

What's that you say? You require further evidence of just how fucked-up the city actually was? Want to know how it felt being surrounded by mobs of unruly Neanderthals hell-bent on looting or burning everything in sight? If anybody needed more verification that the dying heart of a once glamorous city was descending into all-out anarchy, it presented itself in the form of two police officers, battered, bloody, running away from a crowd of brick-throwing youths. One of the constables paused to catch his breath, and glanced over at the purring Pickup. He waved his hand exaggeratedly and pointed in the same direction Ethan had just come from.
"What does he want?" Karris asked, chewing fingernails.

Ethan frowned and looked into the rear-view mirror. "He's telling us to turn around.
"We need help."

"I think they do, too."

"What are we going to do?"

"Hold on."

Bringing the Pickup to a temporary halt in the middle of the sea of juvenility, Ethan attempted a three-point-turn. It was no good. There were too many people blocking him in. He parped the horn, but it was pointless. For all the

good it did him he might as well just get out and politely ask them to move.
Lincoln was screaming hysterically. He was strapped in the backseat, legs not touching the floor, red-faced, tears gushing down crinkled features, voice painfully hoarse. The poor boy must have been terrified. After all, the boy's father was terrified!

There was a loud clank from the back of the truck. Somebody had been shoved hard into the side of the Pickup. Karris gasped loudly. Lincoln stared into the pandemonium with bleary eyes. Ethan revved the engine, and palmed the horn once more.

A hooded yob slammed his fist down on the bonnet.

"Move out of the bloody way!"

"What are we going to do?" Karris asked, aware that he had no answer.
"Just keep calm, yeah?"

Suddenly the Pickup was rocking on its suspension as they tried to tip it over.
"We need to get out!" Ethan roared. "They're tipping the truck!"
Karris nodded her head and quickly unclipped her seat belt.
Ethan shed his own harness and reached in the back for his frenetic son, kicking open the driver's door. Immediately his nostrils were assaulted by the pungent stench of petrol and smoke and tear gas.

Behind him, the Pickup juddered and rolled on its suspension.

It won't take this lot long to overturn the truck!

There was a distinct spiciness in the atmosphere, a noticeable reek. It ambled just beneath the Molotov cocktails and burning buildings; faint, faded, but there all the same. Ethan immediately recognized it for what it was – fever! Yes, these people were undoubtedly sick, but it was an infection of city-crushing devotion which pulsated through their bodies and electrified their hearts, leaving them with no other option than to erupt and vent that fury. Born and bred into a broken city; labelled the root cause, left to fester in squalid conditions, forgotten about unless blame needed to be placed, unable to afford food or pay their bills, depending on food banks, hardly any jobs of any description due to the Prime Minister's brutal cuts, benefits constantly being reduced, council houses continually handed to foreigners who refused to speak our language or believe in our beliefs or support our soldiers, but were happy enough to claim a flood of our benefits. If they had no wage – how were they supposed to put food in their baby's belly?
Ethan paused briefly and looked around. The small butchers to his left was being brutalised by fire. It had already spread to the hairdressers next door. The bay window had shattered from the corroding heat. He looked across the bobbing heads of the crowd and to his right he could see the Curry Mile – a stretch of pizzerias, curry houses, kebab shops, burger bars, tapas restaurants, and chip shops running parallel with the road for an entire mile. Ethan blinked rapidly, smoke mocking his vision, but it looked like the owners and workers were standing outside the shops. And it looked like they had taken it upon themselves to protect their property with a variety of knives, cleavers, and baseball bats. There must have been around a hundred Turkish people - predominately male -

standing there; a confrontation simmering but not quite cooked yet. He'd seen similar things during the London riots a few years back – factions of young men coming together and forming inaccessible circles of protection around their homes and businesses. And who could blame them? Apart from the two police officers fleeing the scene, he hadn't seen a flutter of authority combating the outburst. Something exploded fiercely a few blocks away.

"There!" Ethan screamed over the clatter of the crowd. "You see it?"
Across the road was a small takeaway. The door leading into the eatery was open and a beaded flyscreen hung over it. There was a small mob of robed men standing in front of the shop, illuminated by shades of bright blue from the neon bulbs of the window. Ethan managed to snatch a glimpse of the shop's name – STAIRWAY TO HEAVEN.

He wasn't really a fan of junk food. Had never been one to gorge on curries and pizzas at the end of a busy week. He didn't like the dreaded bloated feeling the following morning or all that garbage barricading his arteries. But he did enjoy the occasional kebab and whenever his appetite craved a Middle Eastern treat smothered in chilli sauce it was always Stairway to Heaven he placed an order with. He was even on first name terms with the proprietor – an arrow-thin Turk named Hassam.
"Come on!"

"What are you thinking?" Karris asked, following her husband's gaze to the takeaway.

"Safety in numbers and all that," he replied, looking anxiously about. "I'm sure Hassam will let me use his phone to call the police."

"Do you think we'll get through?"

Ethan shrugged his shoulders. "We are reporting a murder."
They slalomed through the crowd, stopping only briefly so he could catch his breath and readjust his hold on his son. The Pickup by now was completely submerged in a hooded sea of brutality. It rolled onto its side, and the sound of the windshield shattering broke his heart.

Keeping one eye on Karris and the other on the rabble all around, he stepped from road to kerb and was just about to enter the kebab shop when a yobbo glugging from a bottle of whiskey stepped in front of him. He was wearing the customary tracksuit (hood obviously up) and a dark body-warmer. There was a bandanna concealing the lower portion of his face. Like a victim of Medusa, the youth stood statue-still. Wide eyes blazed and he was blatantly high on destruction.
Intentionally blocking their way into the eatery, Ethan tried sidestepping him. The youth moved with him, dancing forlornly to a ballad of disarray.
"Can I just get past there, mate?" Ethan asked. He tried to keep his voice steady and outgoing.

The yob leered at him.

Karris stepped up beside her husband. She was breathing as though she was under water.

"What you say, blood?" the youth snarled.

"We're just trying to get past," Ethan answered, aware his tone was bordering between sociable and pleading.

"Is this your whore?" the ruffian asked. He said this but it sounded more like diss. He pointed a leather-swathed finger at Karris.

"Hey! There's no need for that!" Ethan quickly reprimanded. "We're just trying to get past. That's all."

"Oh, sure, I'll let you pass," the tearaway sneered. "Once she shows me her tits."

A seed of detestation began to bloom inside Ethan's stomach. Palms absorbed fingernails. From beside him, he heard Karris breathing shakily.

"Go to hell."

"You're already there, man."

Ethan stepped in front of the youth, eyes wide, top lip quivering, ear-piercing screams of his son galloping a relay around his brain.

How dare this haughty little shit insult Karris like this!

Sensing a confrontation simmering between the two men and desperate to avoid it, Karris stepped in front of her husband and lifted her top, displaying the red lace bra retaining her heaving breasts. Due to the circumstances, her boobs were clammy with perspiration, and the young kid was tempted to reach out with both hands and squeeze them roughly.

That seed of detestation bloomed into a desert flower of rage.

The youth laughed and disappeared back into the crowd.

Karris shuddered and pulled her top down.

"Come on," Ethan hissed. "Let's go."

Together they stepped into the takeaway.

CHAPTER 12

He'd always been a lucky son of a bitch.

Back when he'd been studying law at Oxford, the night before his final exam, Bryan had gone partying with a group of Fresher's and had got so annihilated on a combination of cheap whiskey and watered-down lager that he'd completely flunked the test. He turned up late, reeking of booze, and had simply decided to wade through the paper as quickly as possible then return to his dormitory and slip into an alcohol-induced coma. But, as luck would have it, when he'd finally received the dreaded results, he was shocked to see not only had he passed 98% of the major – he'd aced it!
On his first date with his future ex-wife, they went to see a rock band at the Town Hall and the pair had heard gunfire when leaving the concert. Two rival gangs were trading lead – thirty-three shots had been fired in total, the police later confirmed – and as the crowd ran for cover, Bryan had been horrified to see blood splattered all over Aiko's stomach. He'd sat her down on the kerb, thinking she was going to die in his arms, but miraculously, the underwire in her bra had deflected the speeding bullet, bouncing it away from her heart. It pulped her right breast, but only caused superficial damage.

He had been backpacking in Japan and had left only three hours before the tsunami destroyed Fukushima; had managed to pass his driving test despite the fact that he'd forgotten to put on his seat belt at the beginning and, after picking up food poisoning in Boston, had been forced to miss the flight which should have taken him to Los Angeles but would have smashed him straight into the South Tower of the World Trade Centre.

He really was a lucky son of a bitch.

So it defied all logic that the great Bryan Locke should be standing in his best friend's hallway, veiled in smoke, surrounded by framed superheroes, staring in disbelief at the dead dog hanging in the front porch. Blood spewed from the laceration that had been jaggedly carved from Bella's throat straight down her sternum and into her belly, turning her stomach into mince. The beagle's steaming innards - grey, glistening, bloated - dangled like grotesque tinsel, pissing caustic acid, looking as though Santa had decided to replace this year's decorations with bloody tampons. He'd never before realized blood had such a coppery stench.

Lee took a cautious step on his brother's front porch. The lifeless dog swayed back and forth, reminding him of the pendulum on a grandfather clock. He aimed the beam of the flashlight up and exposed the clothesline used to bind Bella's back legs together. He grimaced when he noticed that they had tried decapitating her first.
"Sick bastards," Bryan whispered.

Lee nodded his head. His grip on the wood tightened.

The visceral inferno in the driveway had died down to a steady bonfire by now. Bright flames still licked the night, reached for the dark heavens, canoodled with them, but much of its ferociousness was beginning to calm. Lee scanned the empty driveway. "I told you I heard something."
Bryan nodded slowly. "This has to be them."

"Definitely,"

Behind the two men, in the kitchen, Belinda could be heard sobbing a prayer. She had been the one to discover the mangled dog. They had left Bella merrily yapping away in the garden while strategizing their next move. It had been no longer than ten minutes since Ethan had left to find help when the doorbell had buzzed again. I think you can imagine the rest.

"Hey, wait a minute," Lee said. He shoved past Bryan and stepped off the porch. "There they are! The little bastards are up there!" Converting the stump of wood into a crude pointer, he trained it on three hooded figures standing at the top of the drive.

"Shit," Bryan cursed. "What now?"

"I've had enough of this bollocks," Lee spat. He stormed from the house and stomped gravel. Wind bellowed noisily in his ears.

Bryan grabbed his best mate's brother by the elbow and reeled him in. "Wait a second."

"Let go of me, Bryan."

"I will. Once you've calmed down."

"I'm warning you—"

"What the hell are you going to do, eh?"

"I...I don't know."

"You don't know? You want to go up there and you don't even know what you'll do?"

"Teach them a bloody lesson, that's what."

One of the hooded shapes laughed hysterically.

"Think about what you're saying here, mate."

"I don't need to."

"Lee, this is crazy."

"Get your fucking hands off me!"

"Just wait here until—"

"Until what? What am I meant to be waiting for, Bryan?" Lee slap-clawed himself free and grabbed a handful of the lawyer's shirt, propelling him against the open front door. Bella's dripping corpse rotated. "The police are not coming! Don't you understand that?" He looked at the blue tarpaulin covering Harold's corpse. "They killed him. Are you not getting that? They killed Harold. I couldn't do anything to stop that. But I can sure as hell do something about this!"
"Lee, please—"

"Look after my Mum."

With that Lee Hardcastle marched purposefully up the sloping driveway, fingers tightly wrapped around the piece of wood. The band of youths watched him approach, observed him the same way a hungry lion observes a meaty antelope.
After closing the front door and applying the deadbolt, Bryan raced into the kitchen to get a better view from the overlooking window. Belinda was still sitting at the table, eyes tightly closed, hands clasped together, breathing

faithful promises of gibberish to God.

Lee's out there! Has she not even noticed?

Bryan leaned over the draining board. It was a struggle to see past the flames and his irradiated reflection, but it looked as though Lee had stopped in front of the feral youths. They appeared to be talking. There was no commotion, no raised voices, no unexpected bouts of violence; even Lee seemed to be keeping calm. He looked to be talking in a quiet, cautious tone.

Is that what all of this needed? Wait a minute, what the hell's that? Shit, two more of them are coming from the side of the house!

Bryan watched helplessly as two youths raced up the driveway towards Lee. From the kitchen window he watched one of them spring forward and punch him in the face. Bryan could actually hear knuckle crunching jaw from inside the house. Then he was shoved square in the back as another kneed him in the gut. Legs buckled, and Lee collapsed on his backside.

Sensing the danger he was clearly in, Lee scrambled quickly to his feet and raised the plank of wood, but another youth – this one about ten years old – jumped up and socked him in the side of the head. Lee refused to go down off a love-tap from a child, but he did drop the wood. It washed away beneath a tide of Nike and Adidas trainers. Somebody pushed their way through the jeering crowd, the frontrunner of these deadbeats, and Lee recognized the acne-riddled face of the youth in the garden, the one who had insulted his sister-in-law. Before he could react, he was dragged to his feet and a barrage of insults and phlegm were spat at him. The youth reached around the back of his jogging trousers and pulled a

heavy-looking handgun from the waistband. Lee's heart lurched with dread, stomach contracting.
Oh my God, he's got a gun! He's got a fucking gun!

Brisket-fists reached and claimed him by the throat, squeezing his oesophagus, then the Beretta was smashed against his skull and the skin split. A single tear of blood sobbed down the side of his face.

Lee began to cry.

There's that bitch that attacked Mum!

She was crouching in front of him, making blubbering noises, extending her lower lip mockingly, rubbing her fingers against her cheeks. The sight of this...this...whore...turned the blood in his arteries to poison.
"What are you looking at?"

Lee winced at how sour her breath was. It smelt like an ashtray. "I'm looking at you, you silly cow."

"What did you call me?"
She stepped closer and raised her tattooed eyebrows.

"I think you heard me perfectly the first—"

A small fist full of sovereigns punched him straight in the mouth, shredding both of his lips. There was enough strength in her pint-sized frame to dislodge his front tooth. The jab took him completely by surprise. The bitch packed the strength of a bare-knuckle traveller. He swayed uncertainly on his feet as she bobbed and weaved like Muhammad Ali in his prime. She commanded something

from the circle forming around him, and then his Foo Fighters T-shirt was literally torn from him. Camera phones came out and began recording the entire thing, degrading him further, storing the assault to download to Facebook at a later time.
"Take off your pants," she commanded.

"No."

The muzzle of the Beretta was pressed against the back of his skull. "She said take your pants off, yeah?" The cretin disengaged the safety. "Now be a good boy and do as you're told or I'll blow your fuckin' head off!"
"There's no need for any of this to be happening."

"She said take your pants off."

"I have money."

"Take them off now!"

Refusing to give them the satisfaction of seeing just how embarrassed and shit-scared he actually was, he unbuttoned his Levis and pulled them down around his ankles, standing in the driveway in just his underwear. The Neanderthals cheered and laughed.

"Yeah...yeah...come on then!" Lee roared defiantly. He held his arms up to the black heavens, looking like a stowaway seeing the British border for the first time. "Come on! Come see what a real man looks like!"

The young girl smiled. "Lose the underwear," she demanded. She folded bony arms over a pathetic cleavage.

Is she kidding?

“Not a chance,” Lee said. He swallowed and tasted bile.

Suddenly she snatched hold of his scrotum and squeezed, hard, making him yowl with pain and yanking him forward at the same time, delivering a head-butt straight to the bridge of his nose. Something unintelligible spilled from between bloody lips, and then he was on his back, gravel embalming his body as they kicked and stomped him. He curled into a tight ball as an avalanche of feet kicked his head and booted him in the back; stomped on his arms, hands, feet, buttocks...everywhere. He felt rough hands rolling him over, yanking down his boxer shorts, whisking them past his knees, forcing them around his ankles. The youth armed with the Beretta crouched beside Lee and snatched his wedding ring off.

“Stand up,” the girl panted. And it was only then that he realized who those rough hands had belonged to.

“Fuck off.”

The muzzle of the handgun was once again pressed against the back of his skull.

“Okay, okay,” he breathed. Painfully, he climbed from knees to bare feet.

“Get hard,” she demanded.

“What?”

“You heard me,” the girl smiled. She ran a fake fingernail teasingly across his exposed penis. “I want you to get hard for me.”

“You people are sick.”

“What’s up, baby,” she purred seductively. “Can you not do it? Am I not fit enough for you?”

“Maybe he needs a hand, Charlotte,” the prick behind leered.

“Is that it, honey? Do you want me to help? Do you want to see my boobs?” She slipped an index finger between her lips and looked at him with dopey eyes. “But I’m only fourteen years old, mister. Please don’t be rough with me.”

For God’s sake!

She reached out and grabbed his penis, masturbating painfully. With the threat of the Beretta still pressed against his skull, Lee closed his eyes and forced himself to drift thirteen years into the past to the night he took his wife’s virginity. A couple of perverse seconds later and he was fully erect.

The mob laughed mockingly.

“Is it money that you want?” Lee mumbled. “If it is, my brother has a fucking shitload in that house. He’s a builder; owns his own business, doesn’t trust banks. There’s a safe. He’s got thousands in there.”

Charlotte’s eyes widened. The Beretta remained firmly pressed against his head.

“Where is it?”

“First, let me go.”

Suddenly he was spun around and the youth with the handgun kicked him full force in the testicles. Lee doubled over, coughing, groaning. Fingers gripped his fringe and snapped his head back viciously. The muzzle was aimed directly at his forehead. "Where's the safe?"

"Please let me go."

"Answer the question then I will."

Lee wiped his nose with the back of his hand. "It's in the cellar."
The youth looked up, eyes seeking approval.

Charlotte nodded obligingly.

The trigger was pulled.

CHAPTER 13

The Stairway to Heaven reeked of garlic. It always did. It didn't matter what time it was or if the hour belonged to day or night the place permanently reeked of garlic.
It was so domineering that even the staff – dressed in red T-shirts, red aprons, and red baseball caps – catering for famished office workers with a lunchtime rumble to sedate, lonely evening diners unable to face another microwave meal for one, or (most commonly) pissed-up revellers returning from a boisterous excursion in town – even they, the backbone of this sparkling gold tooth amongst cavities reeked of garlic. The more overbearing aromas of grilled meat and burnt charcoal did very little to camouflage its pungency. The front and back doors were propped open all year round and still the reek lingered.

Ethan Hardcastle pushed the beads of the flyscreen apart and drove his family inside; freighting cargo, hauling the human road train, and straightaway the expected reek saturated him. To be honest, it was a welcome alternative to smoke and disruption. Ethan nodded to the terrified-looking worker behind the counter and looked over to Hassam, who was emptying the register into a cloth money bag.
"Hassam," Ethan panted. He stepped in front of the refrigerated counter. "I need your help." He was surprised to see the refrigerator barren of salad and condiments. Usually there were columns of lettuce and cabbage and sweetcorn arranged neatly beside the bottles of ketchup and mustard and mayonnaise.
Why should something so minor bother you?

He didn't know. And he wasn't about to waste time finding out.

Harold's dead, your Mum's a traumatised wreck, and your wife just got fondled by a fifteen year old schoolboy while you stood by and watched, you useless prick!
He promptly banished it from his mind and got back into the game.
"Ethan?" Hassam was clearly surprised to see the builder and his family out on such a dangerous night. "What are you doing here?"
The proprietor walked towards the counter, and Ethan noticed he had the money bag in one hand and a huge carving knife in the other. The young employee made a sound like he was about to vomit.

"I need your help, Hassam."

"It's not safe to be on the streets."

"I know. I need to use your phone. I have to call the police."
"Are you okay?"

"Please, I really need to use your phone."

"It's not working, the lines are jammed."

Ethan traded apprehensive glances with Karris, and then lifted the hatch leading behind the counter. Here there was a metal table usually used to store pizza boxes and hamburger cartons. Tonight it was home to a crowbar and baseball bat.
Like a butterfly's flapping wings, Ethan Hardcastle's brown irises fluttered from the grimy linoleum beneath his boots to the finger-smudged mirrored walls where a dog-eared leaflet informed him that the rock band Rainmaker were performing at the Playpen tomorrow night. He took

it all in: the coils of sticky fly tape pinned to the ceiling, the hundreds of bristly corpses glued there, the digital menu board (unsurprisingly turned off) mounted above the counter. He'd been to the takeaway on many occasions over the years, but not once had he ever seen it in such a bedraggled state. "What are we going to do?" Karris asked. "If the phones aren't working then how are we going to report Harold's death?"

Hassam looked up, eyes wide, unblinking.

"My stepfather was murdered tonight by arseholes just like these." He crooked a thumb towards the opened door. "I need to contact—"

Suddenly a calamity of rubber-soled feet rebounding off concrete filled the takeaway. Ethan looked towards the opened door in time to see an asteroid of juvenility roll past. A young lout poked his balaclava-wrapped head through the flyscreen and hurtled a bombardment of racist abuse, his bigoted companions making monkey noises or pounding the window. Ethan pulled Karris towards him, gift wrapping her in his thick arms. Hassam shouted something in Turkish; a carton of brown slop thumped against the window as a response. Karris yelped. Ethan felt his heart lurch.

"These idiots are destroying their own city!" Hassam shouted. He slapped the top of the glass counter in frustration. "I am sorry about your loss, Ethan. Really, I am. My cousin Raif called earlier and said these bastards barged into his store and smashed it up. Can you believe that?"

Ethan glanced nervously over his shoulder to make sure the yobs had gone. He opened his mouth to speak, but Hassam beat him to the finish line.

"They poured vodka over his pregnant fiancée. They said they were going to set her on fire! What kinds of cowards do such a thing? She's a pregnant woman!" Hassam's face distorted with rage. He looked as though somebody was tattooing his heart.

A flash of electric blue light fluttered into the takeaway. Ethan turned on his heels, hoping against hope to see a wave of armoured goliaths boring through the abusive crowd. But the thunderous belch of an air-horn quite literally extinguished his hopes of liberation. The fire engine was motionless; standing in the middle of a rampaging horde, a seemingly endless supply of bricks bouncing off its side.

Ethan pressed himself against the wall as something rebounded off the window of the shop. His heart was pounding, lungs working overtime. All around the wedged vehicle, cars and wheelie bins burned. But this red protagonist – a celebrated paladin renowned for battling volatile combustions and equipped with enough paraphernalia to douse the carnage – refused to evict a single fire-fighter. Ethan poked his head through the beaded curtain and counted about fifteen burning cars in the wasteland.

He stepped back from the doorway when he spotted a flock of feral youngsters marching towards the shop, shouting, making hand gestures. Ethan closed the door and sealed them in, cursing when he realized there was no way of locking them out. He was about to ask for the key when one of the hooligans launched something against the window. Thankfully the glass survived, but the noise it made testified under oath that it wasn't prepared to sustain such abuse.

The looters managed to wedge the driver's door of the fire engine open and the poor driver was plucked out like giblets, tossed into the rioting horde like the name etched

on the back of his flight-jacket read REGINALD DENNY. Mortified, Ethan watched as the group punched and kicked him beneath their rubber hooves. Another fire-fighter heroically leaped to his companion's aid, but was greeted with a metal pipe or a crowbar to the jaw. He crumbled to the ground, yellow helmet rolling free.
A barrage of clenched fists slammed against the window of the Stairway to Heaven. Ethan backed away, tripping over his own feet, landing on the filthy linoleum, door handle pressing down, forcing him to spring forward, scrambling on hands and knees, throwing his entire body headfirst into the PVC door. It slammed shut with a perforating bang!
"Take Lincoln in the back!" Ethan ordered. Gloved hands repeatedly pounded the glass above his head. The left side of his face and body had to intermingle with the door, but even then, he barely managed to keep the rabble outside.

"What about you?" Karris shouted. She moved behind the counter.
"I'll be fine," he hoped. "Where's the fucking key?"

Hassam was standing behind the counter, looking like a D-Day veteran returning to the Normandy beaches for the first time; eyes wide, hands clasped together, fingers entwined like star-struck lovers on a midsummer's night. The hinge keeping his mouth closed released its final screw, and his jaw dropped open comically. He glanced nervously towards the crowbar.

Outside, the crew renewed their efforts to gain entry.

"I need the key!" roared Ethan.

Karris raced past a line of industrial ovens and disappeared into the storeroom. She returned a second later, face flushed, hair crimped with perspiration. “There’s a backdoor!”

Thank God! We’ll be able to take the backstreets to Dave’s flat!
“The key,” Ethan screamed. “Where’s the fucking—”

His entire body rattled and he was shoved unceremoniously forward. Deep-seated hands grabbed hold of him. He instinctively pushed backwards, barging the partition painfully on groping fingers, fear topping up his reserves, but it was no good. They were nearly inside.

What the hell do they want? What the hell will they do?

A young boy – about five years older than Lincoln – practically tunnelled his way beneath legs and almost made it inside, but Hassam and his employee jumped over the counter just in time and smashed into the door. The thug screamed, caught like a trout in a net. Remorselessly, he was squashed between the door and wall. A medley of gloved hands ceaselessly tried retrieving him.

“Help me!” he pleaded. “Help me, please!”

Hassam and his worker applied more pressure. Ethan looked down and a raindrop of guilt saturated him. The kid (and that was all he was) was red-faced, breathing like a stuck pig, the door shoving deeper into his ribs, making him cry out in agonized agony. Hassam pulled a ring of keys from his trousers and penetrated the lock even though the door wasn’t completely closed yet.

The air horn mounted to the fire truck belched again.

A flurry of lawbreakers stampeded from the opposite end of the high street carrying carpets, trainers, jewellery, whatever they could, and ploughed straight into the human roadblock outside the kebab shop. The outburst of lawlessness had urged all colours and creeds to become embroiled in the anarchy. Ethan gritted his teeth and glanced over at his crying wife and son.

"When I pull the door open I want you to drag him inside," Ethan said to Hassam.
The owner of the takeaway stared at his loyal customer as though he had just propositioned him for sex. "What?"

"We don't have a choice. We're going to kill him if he stays stuck there for much longer.
"That's his fucking problem!"

"He's stuck between the door and the wall, yeah? That's going to provide them with the advantage. They'll get in."

"I don't want him in my shop!"

"Better one than fifty!"

Ethan nodded. The door pulled back a fraction, catching the horde by surprise, and the youth was pulled kicking, screaming, and spitting into the shop before all three men charged the door closed. The key already occupied the lock, and trembling fingers twisted it. A loud click confirmed the door was secured.

The lout clambered to his knees, dregs of palpitating adrenaline being replaced by fear now that he realized he

was trapped and outnumbered. Holding battered (possibly broken) ribs and with bloody saliva sliding down his scraped chin, the youth nervously glanced around for a possible escape route. Ethan felt his stomach tighten and his testicles lift as he watched the boy still determined to be a man despite the tears gluing his eyelids together and trickling down his flushed cheeks.
The builder released a heavy breath, allowing his head to press against the cool glass of the door.

"What...what do we do...now?" Hassam panted. He was bent at the hip, head down, breathing haggardly, and hands resting on his knees. He looked and sounded as though he had just completed a global marathon. "I don't know," Ethan confessed breathlessly. "I suppose we wait for the police to show up. There's nothing else we can do."
"Wait for the police to show up?" Hassam laughed sarcastically. "There are no police!"

"What do you mean?"

Enraged wolves growl less.

"There are no police! Not anymore!"

Hassam slipped behind the counter and dusted himself down, mopping beads of perspiration from his forehead with a grubby handkerchief, mumbling in Turkish. Ethan watched as he yanked the door of the cooler open and pulled out a can of cola, closing the door with his stick-thin hip. "And what are we supposed to do with him?" He pointed a bony finger towards the sniffling youth, but the question was directed at Ethan.

Stepping behind the counter and accepting his son, kissing Lincoln's head, reassuring the toddler that everything was going to be fine, Ethan stared Hassam directly in the eye. "I don't know. I don't have any answers."

"I told you that I didn't want him in my shop!" Hassam said. He uncapped the cola with a loud tzzzz, cursing as fizzy soda ejaculated all over his hand.

The roaring crowd surrounding the shop dispersed down the high street, apparently accepting the loss of one of their own and moving on to cause more disruption. The congregation clapped and cheered when they came across a petrified Turkish man on the verge of a heart attack, sprinting down the street, nose streaming with blood, slicked back hair windblown. Bizarrely he had no trousers on. His white shirt was stained with blood and smoke. Apart from that he was wearing nothing but shoes over ankle socks. His shirttails flowed like a superhero's cape as he ran down the street, one hand clearing a path through the laughing mob, the other trying to cover his manhood. Ethan unlocked the door with the attentiveness of a crocodile tamer and stepped outside. The crying yobbo with the extremely bruised ribs moved forward, sensing possible freedom, but Hassam pushed him firmly back.

"Hey!" Ethan bellowed. "Over here! Over here!" He waved his arms above his head as though landing a Boeing aeroplane.

The scared-stiff Turk stopped and, gasping for breath, looked towards Ethan. He reminded Ethan of a frightened rabbit having just heard the first bloodcurdling bark of a hunting dog.

"Hurry up!" Ethan shouted. He cupped both hands in front of his mouth. "Hurry up before they come back!"

Hassam shoved past Ethan, holding the youth by the scruff of his coat and, glaring at Ethan, shoved him squarely between the shoulder blades, pushing him away from the shop. Ethan frowned. The kid looked shocked, quickly erecting his hood and racing after his comrades. He had gone no further than a couple of paces before he stopped, refilled to the brim with arrogance, and saluted the two men with his middle finger. The owner of the Stairway to Heaven looked over at his fellow Turk and shouted something in their native tongue. The semi-naked man hesitated for no more than a split-second before replying with one word, and disappearing down a frightfully black alley.
“What did he say?” Ethan asked.

Hassam shook his head. “What he said makes no sense.”

“Why?”

“He said saytan,”

“What does that mean?”

Hassam looked down at the floor.

“It’s Turkish for demons.”

CHAPTER 14

Belinda Hardcastle charged into Bryan Locke, boosting him backwards, propelling him against the front door, screaming into his face.

How can a sixty-eight-year-old woman possess so much strength?

Bryan gritted his teeth. He refused to let her barge past, wincing as fingernails clawed his face, small fists bashing his chest. He smothered her hands in his own and pulled her towards him, absorbing her insults, enduring her wrath, blocking her path like an insistent branch of a forming dam. He hated this! He hated having zero control over a situation offering no answers. There was no excuse for these louts to be attacking them. Poor Lee had been beaten and shot! What had they achieved? They had killed Bella, severed the poor dog from throat to groin her up by the legs, but why? What had they gained? What could they gain? Belinda went for the door again. This time Bryan dispensed all his strength, heaving her back into the kitchen.

"You can't go out there," said Bryan. He figured that wrestling her through the doorway was probably the equivalent of pushing a wardrobe upstairs single-handedly. "I'm sorry, I really am, but they're still out there." Quivering fingers clicked the fluorescents off. Blackness flooded the bungalow. Tongues of flame pirouetted through the kitchen window and provided Bryan just enough light to see the bastards outside.

"He's dead, isn't he?" Belinda sobbed into another sopping handkerchief. Bryan didn't know where she was getting them from. "They've killed him. I can feel it." She patted just above her broken heart. "I can feel it in here."

Bryan crossed to the window and peered outside. The throb of his distraught heart increased as he saw the youths striding down the driveway towards the house.
Five! There are five of the little shits!

Stealthily, he crossed the kitchen and snatched a bread knife from the block.
"He's dead. I know he is."

"Belinda," hissed Bryan. "Not now, okay?"

"I know. Trust me, I know."

Bryan thought it best to keep his mouth closed.

"Why are they doing this?"

"I don't know. We just need to stay here until the police or Ethan turn up."
"And what if Ethan doesn't make it back?" A flotilla of fear launched another strike against her ruptured heart. "Or what if he makes it all the way back and they do the exact same thing to him as they did to Lee? I could lose two sons in one night!"
"You can't think like that."

A giggling lout rapped his knuckles against the front door, knocking as casually as a FedEx deliveryman. A hooded silhouette peered through the kitchen window, his gloved goblets covering the sides of his face. He squinted into the dark kitchen. Belinda gasped loudly. Bryan pressed a finger to her lips to silence her.
The scraggy girl crouched in front of the door and lifted the letterbox, shushing her jeering comrades. "Cooooooeeee!" she called through the mail-slot. "This is

Avon calling!"

Knuckles clapped gently against the window again. Bryan had to press up against the refrigerator to avoid being seen. He whispered over to Belinda to find a similar source of cover. Laughter boomed from outside. Something heavy struck the front door, could have been the same brick used to kill Harold, Bryan really didn't know. Belinda stifled a scream and waddled into the doorway. Bryan raised a hand, gesturing for her to remain quiet. Something bounced off the door again. Bryan could swear he heard the wood crack. Trickling, followed by raucous laughter, and then the vile stench of urine wafted into the house. Bryan closed his eyes, throat constricting to the size of a pinhead, hands shaking uncontrollably, the handle of the knife growing slippery in his grasp. He heard more calling. More insults. And then something was launched through the kitchen window.

Bryan grabbed Belinda by the hand and towed her out of the kitchen, down the hall, into the living room, closing the door behind him as the sound of adolescent feet scuttled into the house. There was only a single corner lamp burning in here, and Bryan quickly flipped it off at the mains. He dragged Belinda to the far end of the room and pushed her in between an armchair and a display cabinet proudly boasting sixty or seventy original Star Wars figurines, reprimanding her when she tried to speak.

From the kitchen, he could clearly hear the repulsive degenerates clambering through the broken window. There was a heavy dunk followed by laughter, and Bryan could only assume one of them had fallen on the draining board. He heard the girl – that bitch – command

something and then one of Ethan's beloved framed comic books was destroyed.
"Listen to me, Belinda," Bryan whispered. "I need you to stay here. I need you to be as quiet as possible."

"They are going to find us," Belinda croaked. "They are going to find and kill us."
"No, that's not going to happen."

"They have a gun."

"Belinda, I won't let them hurt you. I promise."

The TV in the corner of the room was still turned on, broadcasting the news to an empty sofa. Low voices, barely audible, drifted across, threatening to expose them. Bryan crept across the room and bent down to unplug it. His eyes fell on the headline rushing across a frozen picture of the second Prince to the Throne, Prince Jasper, and his beautiful fiancée, Adela. The headline on the TV read BREAKING NEWS: PRINCE JASPER BEATEN TO DEATH BY LOOTERS INSIDE BUCKINGHAM PALACE.
Bryan felt his bowels loosen. He inhaled a shaky breath as the caption beneath revealed PRIME MINISTER ROBERT HARRIS CONTEMPLATING MARTIAL LAW.

"Bryan?" Belinda whispered from her couching position. "Bryan? What's wrong?"
"Nothing," hissed the lawyer. He quickly turned the TV off and tiptoed over to the door. He hid behind it, feeling very much like a five-year-old boy playing hide-and-seek with his sister. The knife in his hand felt absurdly heavy. He could feel bile sloshing around in his gut. He had been

acquainted with fear before, but not on this level. He closed his eyes and saw his mother.

“Are they in the house?”

“Shut up.”

"I’m scared, Bryan.”

“Me too,”

Suddenly, footfalls dragged into the living room and Bryan held his breath, certain that his clonking heart beat was going to betray him. He could hear raspy breathing, but the door concealed the hooded menace from view. He glanced in the direction of Belinda. Thankfully she had the sense to keep down.
“Where are they?” someone shouted from the kitchen.

Fingertips gripped the edge of the door. The blade of the bread knife was raised.
“Charlotte? Where the fuck did they go?”

Wind blustered over the roof, jigging slates, sounding like a pissed-off Chupacabra.
He heard movement directly in front of him. Lungs threatened to rupture.
“There’s no one in here.”

The words were like a red flag to an irate bull. As soon as Belinda heard that malicious little squawk’s voice, she rose, slowly, deliberately, stepping from beside the display cabinet like the clichéd serial killer in a bad horror movie; silent, motionless, intimidating. Then the young girl turned around...and wished she hadn’t.

Belinda rushed forward with a speed which belied her years and the grace of an assassin, grabbing the lapels of Charlotte's jacket, pulling her forward, pushing her onto the sofa, and landing on top of her. The young girl tried to scream, desperate to alert her companions, but Belinda slapped her once across the face. The strike was astonishingly loud in the catacomb and Bryan moved from behind the door just as a boy, no older than ten, stepped through the doorway.

The boy paused when he saw Bryan. The little fucker even managed a smile, until he saw the knife. The blade glinted, and the boy turned on his heels, but Bryan was too fast, grabbing his hood, yanking it down, revealing his infantile face, throwing him through the doorway, cartwheeling over the puffet, slamming down onto the boy's back.

Belinda looked over to Bryan. Her eyes were red-rimmed, wide, and apologetic, granting Charlotte one of her three wishes, which she took. Elbow crunched jaw. The older woman was tossed aside, weight advantage quickly losing out to youth. Charlotte jumped off the sofa and released the scream buzzing around her lungs. Bryan turned around just as she charged into him.

A flurry of fists bombarded his face. He tried defending himself, but the little fucker on the floor was up, jumping on his back, strangling, choking, biting, and Bryan was kicked between the legs with as much ferociousness as Lee had been earlier. Knees buckled. He collapsed into a crumpled heap. Feet and fists escorted his descent. From far away, but no more than a few inches, he heard the girl screaming, "In here, they're in here," and then Belinda screamed feverishly. The girl spoke no more.

Through a barrier of his own arms and hands, he looked into darkness and saw Charlotte stumble drunkenly

towards him. Her face was pale, deathly pale, and when her lips opened a dribble of black blood trickled down her chin. Her scraped-back hair had become untangled during the scuffle, revealing the full length and aura of her mane, baring hidden innocence. When she opened her arms and reached out for him, he saw the handle of the bread knife protruding from between two undeveloped breasts. A geyser of blood spewed out from around the hilt.
"Help...help...please..."

Bryan jumped to his feet and reached for the young girl.

"Leave her," Belinda commanded from behind. "Leave her."
"Belinda, what the hell have you done?"

Charlotte staggered like a baby giraffe and collapsed backwards, arms outstretched, groping, legs sprawling, the back of her skull cracking against the corner of the coffee table. The boy made an attempt to dash through the opened doorway, but Bryan grabbed a handful of his coat and pretended not to notice the stench of hot urine wafting from the crotch on the boy's trousers.

"The same thing those little bastards did to my Harold. The same thing they did to my son!"

"I can't condone this. I can't condone...this."

"Then don't."

"You fucking killed her!"

"There was no other choice."

"No, no, you're wrong. There are always choices."

Belinda stepped forward. Her eyes showed no remorse.

"There was no other choice."

Suddenly, a barrage of stampeding youths raced down the hall leading into the front room, shouting, cursing, and threatening. Bryan slammed the door shut on them, heaving the sideboard behind it just as shoulders began batter-ramming from the opposite side. The boy screamed for help. Belinda socked his mouth closed with an open-palmed slap.

Bryan stepped over the dead girl in the centre of the room and pulled the curtains apart, revealing the backdoor which would lead into the yet-to-be-constructed conservatory, which in turn led onto to the back garden. Sweaty fingers grasped the door handle, pressing down, yanking it from its hinges nearly, stumbling outside, pulling Belinda behind him, and closing the door on the boy, leaving him sobbing in the bungalow.

I know it's a long-shot, but if we can make it over the fence and onto the moors before they break the door down then maybe, just maybe—

The helicopter dropped from the black heavens like a stone being dropped from the Eifel Tower. It roared above the bungalow, circling it, dropping lower. The huge spotlight mounted to the underbelly illuminated Bryan and his best mate's mother. Bryan ran into the middle of the lawn and raised his arms, pleading for help despite the fact that the enormous propellers chopping the wind made it impossible for anybody to hear anything. He glanced back towards the house, but no longer felt the same cocktail of fear and dread pumping through his body. Either Ethan had managed to contact the police or they had shown up on their own accord. It didn't really matter either way.

The little bastard in the front room had dislocated the sideboard far enough for his three comrades to barge their way into the room. Bryan, mortified, watched as the leader of these hooded minions, the deadbeat with the Beretta, crouched beside Charlotte's dead body, cradling her, stroking her hair. The blubbering boy pointed furiously towards the garden.

The helicopter hovered directly over the house. Bryan and Belinda were cascaded in a circle of bright light. It was only then that Bryan realized it wasn't a police helicopter, as first assumed, but a military 'copter of some description. The side door was pulled back and an armed soldier looked down below.

"We're saved!" Belinda screamed. A flicker of a smile flashed across her face. "They're here to save us!"

Bryan looked up at the chopper once more, studied the soldier strapped in the doorway. Even though the visor of his tactical helmet concealed his eyes, Bryan couldn't shake the feeling that they were trained on him. Despite the ear-splitting holler of the 'copter's rotating propellers, Bryan could clearly hear the back door being flung open; could hear the sound of the safety being removed from the Beretta. He turned and watched the youth stagger outside. He repeatedly rubbed tears from his face with the back of his hand.

"You killed her!" he bawled. "You fucking killed her!"

His finger flirted outrageously with the trigger.

Bryan held his hands above his head, looking like a hostage in a bank siege. Belinda did the same.

Overhead, the helicopter circled the house once more. "Nobody else has to die tonight!" Bryan roared. Courageously, he stepped forward. "Too many people have lost their lives already."

"She was my sister!" the youth screamed. His voice cracked with a sob. Tears rolled down flushed cheeks. The remaining mob pushed through the doorway, creating a defensive line.

From the soaring helicopter above, the robotic voice of the pilot spewed into a megaphone: "PUT THE GUN DOWN!"

The youth ignored the order. He kept the muzzle pointed directly at Bryan's head.

"You killed my sister!"

Belinda stepped forward. "You killed my fiancé! You killed my son!"

The Beretta was switched from lawyer to mother.

"Look," Bryan shouted, "nobody else needs to die tonight. No more blood needs to be spilled."

One of the hooded youths stomped across the patio and trod onto the lawn, stepping up beside the armed teenager.

The helicopter repeated its instruction again.

"Blood, what the hell're you waitin' for?" the youth asked. "Fuckin' pop 'em both and let's go!"

"No!" pleaded Bryan. "It doesn't have to end this way!"

"What're you waitin' for, Kieran? They murdered Charlotte, yeah? Are you just gonna allow 'em to get away with it? Are you seriously gonna look a pussy in front of your boys?"

"Shut up, Calum! Everybody just shut the fuck up!"

"PUT THE GUN DOWN! THIS IS YOUR FINAL WARNING! PUT THE FIREARM DOWN NOW!"

Kieran pushed his hood free and revealed his features for the first time. Clean-shaven, cropped hair, skin pockmarked from a lengthy battle with acne, but he looked no different to Bryan's nephew, lecturing computer-programming at Harvard. He didn't look like a monster. He looked like a grieving brother who had just discovered the blood-splattered body of his cherished sister.

In a heartbeat, Bryan predicted what was about to happen next, and launched himself into Belinda, rugby tackling her, propelling them both into the shrubbery at the bottom of the garden as the M60 opened fire. At precisely the same time, Kieran fired too. Twenty-three hollow-pointed cartridges fired from the machine gun in a matter of seconds, each round remarkably precise, pumping into the seventeen-year-old body of Calum Korini, pulping his heart into paper-mâché; slaughtering, tearing lungs to ribbons, leaving him lifeless on the patio.

Kieran had managed to fire two bullets before sprinting back inside the house. The first bullet pinged off the side of the 'copter, minor scarring, but the second bullet - the luckier one - crashed through the windshield, obliterating it, driving straight into the unprotected jaw of the pilot. The pilot sprawled lifelessly onto the controls, spinning the helicopter. It dipped forward at an incredible angle; spinning propellers chopping the nearest trees like spinach in a blender, then it turned sideward, defying all navigational logic, roaring over the roof of the bungalow, spinning with epileptic speed, soaring towards the stretching moors.

A second later and the thunderous explosion – boom – followed by a mushroom cloud of undiluted fire sealed the fate of not only the poor soldiers on board, but also that of Bryan and Belinda.

CHAPTER 15

Ethan Hardcastle slammed the side of his fist against the front door and stepped back on the veranda. He peered over the wrought iron railings into the black bowels of the three-storey apartment complex. Karris was standing beside him, cloaked in shadows, Lincoln in her arms and stretching muscles she didn't even know existed. Lincoln was awake now, witnessing everything, but at least he'd stopped crying. In fact, after leaving the Stairway to Heaven and taking the back streets to Dave's flat, Karris had even managed to convince him that what was happening was one big game – like in the Power Rangers when Emperor Gruumm tries to invade Earth only to be beaten by the good guys every time. As she had told him this, a body doused in flames ran screaming across the alleyway, arms flailing, lungs seared, and Ethan had stopped and hushed them quiet by placing a finger to his lips. He had pulled them down behind an overflowing wheelie-bin, and a second later, a group of youths had followed the flaming trail, splitting their sides laughing, recording it on their phones.

"Mummy, are they the bad guys?" Lincoln had innocently whispered. Thankfully, the wheelie-bin had blocked both his eyes and nose. Karris had nodded slowly and tried to control the quiver in her voice. "Yes, baby. They are the bad men."

Five minutes later and the smoky alleyway rolled towards a swanky-looking apartment block; congested council bins replaced by padlocked storage units; neatly trimmed hedges; where tarmac superseded gravel. Ethan had thumbed the intercom in front of the bright yellow retainer barrier and waited anxiously whilst his brother allowed him access. There was usually a burly security guard standing in the doorway of a Portakabin, either smoking or thumbing through a newspaper, but tonight the door was padlocked from the outside. The retainer barrier automatically raised and, carrying Lincoln in one hand and an offering from Hassam in the other, Ethan stepped into the hidden fortress. His boots noisily crunched the loose pebbles stretching from the gateway to the front lobby.

"Dave!" Ethan fingered the mail-slot open and bellowed into his brother's apartment. "Dave, it's me, Ethan, open up!"

From far away, somebody screamed. The rattle of gunfire silenced them.

Ethan offered his son a reassuring smile, the gesture feeling tight and fake. Karris opened her mouth to say something when the slam of the lobby door closing made her heart jump into her throat. Fingernails sank into the flesh of his forearm. Ethan looked up to see Karris nodding towards the dimly-lit stairwell. He frowned and Karris jiggled her head once more. Silently, he crossed to the railings and glanced cautiously over. The two hooded youths conversing in the foyer made his knees weaken.

How have they got in here?

There had been nobody loitering around the grounds when the retainer gate had been raised. Did that mean somebody else had allowed them in? Maybe one of the tenants on one of the other two levels, perhaps?

Surely not! No one in their right mind would fraternize with these crazy criminals, would they? Not in these luxurious apartments!

Ethan heard movement on the stairs, gazed over the railings, and saw two figures dashing up the stairwell. They were obviously aroused by his raised voice. No point trying to keep quiet now. His hollering had been loud enough to wake the dead. Instead, he stepped in front of the door and rattled it another three times.

Dave Hardcastle opened the front door and pushed the screen door aside. He looked warily around the gloomily lit corridor before joining his brother on the veranda. There were another three or four equally lavish apartments on this level, but either they were up for let or the tenants had decided to seek safety elsewhere. Windows were lifeless, black, no noise coming from any of the apartments.

That doesn't mean a thing, though. With everything that's going on, I wouldn't be surprised if they weren't in the living room, huddled together, watching the world slip further into Hell's grip. That's what I'd be doing if I was at home...

home…

...suddenly he was back home, looking at Harold's dead body, listening to his grieving mother howl, sob, and then the relief at being here, in the complex with Dave, washed over him, overwhelmingly reassuring. He was transferred twenty-five years into the past, to the day he had gotten into a scrap with a fat kid at school called Anthony Render. That morning, at the back of the school's woodwork classroom, Ben Leister, Ethan's best friend, a gangly prawn of a lad, had been beaten senseless by Anthony because Ben had scored a goal past him in P.E. the day before. Anthony had taken this blatant insult personally and really went to town on the poor lad, beating him bloody and leaving Ethan with no other option but to intervene and break up the one-sided fight. A hyped-up battle had then been booked straight after school at the back of the old social club and Anthony's nose had been broken during the skirmish. The chubby kid and his plump cronies had jumped on Ethan like deprived bloodhounds, proceeding to kick seven shades of the brown stuff out of him. At some point word floated across the old railway track and reached the counter of the supermarket where Dave had worked. The oldest of the three Hardcastle brothers heroically vaulted the counter and barged through the door, sprinting to his brother's aid and charging into Ethan's attackers. Bricks and threats had been thrown. The bullies had never bothered Ethan again. And Dave had cemented himself as a father figure to the boy; a sentinel of muscle, a tower of protection.

The tiny island of hair at the back of Dave's balding head was unkempt and messy, and he hadn't shaved in a while. There was at least five days' worth of whiskers protruding from his jaw. He wore burgundy corduroys and a white long-sleeved turtle-neck. The sleeves were rolled up to reveal ridiculously hairy forearms. By the look of his unruly beard and the reservoir of follicles on his arms, Ethan wondered how covetously resentful his head must have been. For some mad reason, this made him want to bellow with laughter.

Dave saw the concern etched on Karris's face, saw his youngest brother looking as glum as Bank Holiday weather, and then he saw the black-handled knife he was holding.

"Ethan? What the hell are you doing—"

Ethan quickly waved him quiet. Karris pointed with a trembling finger to the stairs.
In the middle of the foyer was a decorative fountain. Two fibreglass dolphins had been suspended above. A pivot in the octangular skyline held them in place and made them sway in mid-air. A timer in the basin was cranked to

release a blast of air every fifteen minutes which would send a geyser of water shooting high into the air for dramatic effect. The weightless dolphins were fitted with solar lights which made them glow purple and yellow come dusk. The attraction was obviously a strategically-placed and aesthetic item from a money-hungry landlord who wanted to effectively capture the roving eye of potential buyers, leaving them with no doubt that this little slice of urbanity was probably as close to the wonderland they were going to get. Lincoln had once invested a tiny fortune of his father's money in the watery depths after Dave had convinced the boy that wishes would be granted for every coin tossed in. He briefly wondered if his son would ever wish for anything but peace and calm ever again.
A black youth about fifteen years old dashed up the dark stairway. He stopped dead on the veranda, wearing a blue Lacoste tracksuit and box-fresh trainers. There was a backward snap-cap baseball cap, and a price tag still pinned to the collar of the tracksuit.

Ethan immediately stepped in front of Karris and their son – his world – prepared to protect them by any means necessary. He pushed the front door of Dave's home wide open and ordered them inside.

Wind roared overhead like a fanatical lion. The unmistakable pitter-patter of rain beginning to fall against a glass skyline filled the silent complex.
Karris stepped between the two brothers and entered the apartment. She stopped in the hallway, refusing to allow the front door to fully close.
Ethan stealthily slipped the blade of Hassam's departing donation down the back of his jeans, folding his arms over his wide chest.

The black youth looked over his shoulder, checking where his companion was, and paused briefly. His eyes switched from Ethan to Dave, Dave to Ethan, and then settled upon the door. A smile – wicked, evil, and ungodly – flashed across his clean-shaven face. Ethan assumed that must have been what Lucifer looked like when he'd decided to cross the boundary of Good to dabble in Evil.

The baseball cap was snatched off. Long braided cornrows were revealed. "Hey, where're you going, baby? The fun's just getting started."

From the gloom of the hallway, Karris could clearly hear the heavy footsteps announcing the arrival of the youth's partner in crime.

"We don't want any trouble," Dave said. He protectively stepped in front of his forty year-old baby brother. "Feel free to take whatever you want from the homes behind me, mine included, but we don't want any trouble." "Shut up, old timer!" a strong cockney accent commanded. There was no mistaking the subculture of this white, painfully-thin man standing before them. Cigarette dangling between lips, bleached jeans, boots, red braces worn in an x-shape over white vest. The skinhead slapped the broad end of a baseball bat into his palm. "You're boring me already!"

"You took your fuckin' time, didn't you? These two could've wasted me."

The cockney skinhead inhaled, hard, and then flicked the cigarette onto the floor. He obliterated it beneath the sole of his boot. "No need to worry about these two. They don't have a fight in 'em."

"Look, we're not interested in what you're—"

Before Ethan could finish, the skinhead sprang forward, Malcolm McDowell style, driving the handle of the baseball bat into the builder's stomach. Wood burrowed into flesh. Ethan fell forwards and landed on his knees, receiving a hefty kick to the same area. Ethan felt as though the air had been literally pulled from his lungs. He slopped onto his back, curling his knees into his stomach.

"You think you're the business, eh? You think you know me? You ain't shit, you hear? We own the streets tonight."

"That's fine with us!" Dave shouted. Heart pounding and with his tongue constantly slipping from his mouth to moisten dried lips, he watched Ethan crawl towards the front door, grunting, in pain, sill determined to defend his family. "Take the streets! Own them for all I care! Just stop with the violence, please!"
"It's not about what you want, you dopey bastard. You people don't have a clue, do you?

"What are you talking about?"

"It's about time you people realized what you're up against."
"Trust me, we're finding out the hard way."

Without warning, the baseball bat swung again. Dave managed to predict then duck, stumbling over his feet and clashing with the railings. The wooden club rained down once more. Dave barely managed to scramble away in time before his skull was fractured. Fingers loosened on the handle as the vibration with the railings bolted pain into the skinhead's hands.
Dave reacted quickly, driving an elbow into his enemy's belly, shoving him back towards the dimly-lit stairwell.

He hoped the little cockney bastard might tumble down, break his neck in the process, but the fucker managed to grab the handrail in time.

Dave roared in agony as the black youth grabbed a handful of his matted mop and snapped his head back. He could hear the hair being torn from his skull. He was pushed back against the railings of the balcony, the youth trading hair for throat, squeezing hard. Dave Hardcastle struggled to breathe, lungs straining. The little fucker craned his neck, making it almost impossible to inhale.

A blast from the fountain showered both men in frothy water.

White light suddenly exploded in front of his eyes, consuming him, blinding him, making his entire body tremble spasmodically. A spark of indescribable peace began to warm him from within. It embraced him, cloaked him, and made breathing no longer laborious. His face was the brightest of reds and his eyes were beginning to bulge, but he no longer cared. Felt no fear. No desire to unclasp those beast-like claws pressing down on his throat. Even with tongue protruding from swollen lips, he did not feel fear. What was there to be frightened of?

Dave closed his eyes and his head lolled to one side. His breathing grew noisy and irregular. The youth squeezed tighter, smelling death in the stale air.

The sobbing heavens exhibited their disapproval with a bellow of thunder.

And then the pressure around his throat released. A tidal wave of oxygen streamed into deflated lungs. White haze dispersed. And then he was falling forwards, knees buckling, crashing onto the floor. The black youth staggered on wobbly legs in front of him, one hand reaching for the banister of the veranda, the other trying the remove the knife lodged between his shoulder blades. His eyes widened with fear, surprise, pain, and then he was suddenly snatched from view, arms thrashing, toppling over the railings, gravity abruptly claiming its victim. He fell three storeys into a watery grave. The fall was quick, death immediate, like if Peter Parker tried scaling the Daily Bugle office without the outfit. His piercing scream echoed through the complex long after his heart had stilled.

Dave felt damp hands under his arms, dragging him, rolling him onto his side, slapping his face, ordering him to wake up. Then the hands disappeared as quickly as they had come. They left behind a slick trail of something on his face. His eyes blinked open and saw Ethan limping towards a confrontation with the skinhead, one arm wrapped around his injured ribs. He was coughing, spitting, and then Dave saw Ethan's hands covered in blood. He didn't know exactly what had happened, but it looked like Ethan had stabbed the knife into the kid's back and the fall had snuffed a fast-fading flame.

The skinhead leaped forward. Shocked at seeing his companion killed before his eyes, he swung the baseball bat again. This time Ethan reacted more quickly, rugby tackling him to the floor, rolling over, scrambling on top of him. Fists shattered teeth. And he punched him again and again and again, splattering the skinhead's nose across his face much like he had splattered Anthony Render's all those years ago. The skinhead's face burst like an infected abscess, but Ethan carried on raining blows. The skinhead gagged on the coppery fluid pouring down his throat.

Then Ethan was off, spinning like an angry scorpion, fingers folding around the handle of the baseball bat. He raised the baton above his head and braced himself to bring it crashing down—

“Ethan! No! Don’t do it!”

Ethan Hardcastle paused, baseball bat above head, and turned towards his wife.
Karris stepped onto the dark veranda.

Dave climbed up from his knees and rubbed at his throat. Red-faced, sweating, froth drying in the corners of his mouth, but at least he was breathing regularly.

“Get out of here, Karris! You don’t have to see this!”

“No! I won’t allow you to do this!”

“They just tried to kill Dave!”

“You’re not like them!”

“They kicked the shit out of me!”

“You’re not like them!”

“I’m the same as them!”

Tears swelled his eyes. A droplet dribbled free and trickled sorrowfully down his cheek. He brushed it away with the back of his hand. When he spoke, it felt as though somebody had replaced his Adam’s apple with a lump of coal.
“I killed him,” he sobbed. “I...killed...him.”

Dave staggered forwards. He stared down at the crumpled skinhead spitting blood and broken teeth onto the floor.

"You did what you had to do, Ethan. You did what Karris and I expected of you. You saved your family. But it has to end here." Pale blue eyes locked onto the raised baton. "Put the bat down. It's over."
Roaring like a Tyrannosaurus Rex with an itchy belly, Ethan brought the baseball bat crashing down on the banister. The wood split in two halves, one half sailing over the veranda and the other thrown into the bloody fountain. He tottered unsteadily over to Karris, cradling bruised ribs, and allowed her loving arms to enfold him. He wailed and howled into her bosom.

Dave pulled the skinhead to his feet by the scruff of his vest. "I suggest you leave before I release his muzzle."

The skinhead offered no resistance, which didn't surprise Dave seeing as the arsehole could barely speak. He merely nodded and glanced down at his dead comrade before limping towards the stairwell.
"Daddy, are you okay?"

Ethan pulled away from Karris and gently pushed her aside. He crouched in front of his son who was now standing in the doorway. "Hey champ," Ethan smiled. He rubbed his eyes, artificially jolly. "I'm okay. It's just been one long night, that's all. It's nothing a cuddle from you won't fix." At the sound of the little boy's voice, the bleeding skinhead stopped and turned. He saw Ethan crouched in front of the toddler, and stumbled forwards. Dave stepped in front of him, placing a hand on the punk's chest. The skinhead swatted it away.

"Don't be afraid, little soldier." Blood spewed from ruptured lips. It stained his chin deep red. He looked like a feasting vampire. "There's nothing to fear anymore."

Ethan sprang to his feet and pushed his son behind him. Fingers curled once more into deadly weapons.

The skinhead swayed unsteadily.

“Don’t talk to him!” Ethan snarled. “Don’t ever talk to my boy!”
Ignoring the builder, the skinhead reeled forward. It looked like he was on the verge of fainting.”

“Who is that man, Daddy?”

“He’s nobody, honey-bear. That man is nobody. Why don’t you and Mummy go inside?”

The skinhead stumbled forward again.

Ethan blocked his path.

“It’s time to rise up, little soldier,” the skinhead hawked. “It’s time to rise as one. Rise against the system!”

Ethan grabbed a handful of the bastard’s grubby vest and pulled the skinhead towards the balcony, pressing him against the railings. “I’m warning you, you filthy fucking scumbag; unless you want to join your friend down there, I suggest you stop speaking to my boy!”

Karris picked Lincoln up and disappeared inside the apartment.
Dave placed a paw on his brother’s shoulder. “Leave now.”
The skinhead took two wary steps backward, turned, galloped down the staircase and dissolved into its gloominess. The slam of the door confirmed his departure.

Ethan waited a second, making sure the fucker had indeed left, then slid down the wall and collapsed onto his arse; knees raised, head buried in bloody hands. Dave stayed a cautious distance, burnishing a tender throat. After a few long seconds he finally spoke. "Why did you come here tonight?"
"Harold's dead," Ethan blurted. There was no "I've got some bad news" or "maybe you should take a seat", nothing like that. Ethan Hardcastle didn't have time for any of that bullshit. What he needed was good old-fashioned honesty.
"What are you talking about?"

"They..." he derailed momentarily. "My house, tonight, it was targeted by a bunch of fucking kids. They beat Harold to death. Mum and Lee are still up there. I can't—"Hey," Dave said. "Calm down, Ethan, calm down. Now what do you mean, Harold's dead?"

"I told you. They killed him."

"Who? Who's they?"

"I don't know." Ethan rubbed bloodshot eyes. "Some kids attacked my house tonight. I don't know why. I don't know who they were. They killed Harold and petrol-bombed his and Lee's cars—"

"What? And you say Mum's still up there?"

Ethan nodded.

"We need to get back there, Eth. We need to go and get Mum."

“That’s why I came here. I thought we stood more of a chance contacting the police if we were in the city.”

“Have you not heard?”

“Heard what?”
Before he could reply, a noise – whirring, wailing, and high-pitched – roared into the complex. It deafened the two Hardcastle brothers. Mournful screeching raised and dropped, making the hair on the back of Ethan’s neck stand to attention. Thunder belched overhead, two ear-splitting planks of sound slamming together, but even that was no competition for the broken-hearted wail of the air raid siren.

CHAPTER 16

The pregnant rain clouds fully dilated at one o'clock in the morning and delivered a drenching offspring onto the crumbling society below. At that precise moment, the British Prime Minister, Robert Harris, had been sitting alone in his study watching events unfold on the news. The storm had really begun to pick up, rare weather intervals with silky-voiced forecasters predicting "torrential downpours" and "hurricane-force winds" over the coming hours. Robert Harris had sipped the whiskey, glancing continuously from TV, to phone, to rain-splattered study window. On a beautiful summer afternoon the viewer would be rewarded with the sight of a neatly-trimmed lawn and lovingly tended flowerbeds. Not tonight, though.

Robert Harris had looked back at the TV, wincing as the fiery fluid scorched his throat, and had watched, helplessly, as a smartly-dressed pensioner about the same age as his father had been beaten by four hooded Asians. The headline on the screen had read BREAKING NEWS: VIOLENT DISTURBANCES HAVE BEEN REPORTED IN EVERY MAJOR CITY IN BRITAIN.

The Prime Minister had climbed to his feet and paced nervously back and forth, mind repetitively replaying the telephone conversation with Lorraine Fielding he had just abruptly ended. He had listened to the wind howl dementedly, listened to rain gush down the steel drainpipe, listened to the TV footage of a blatantly rattled Mayor of London condemning these senseless riots as "acts of stupidity by cowardly culprits."

Bare feet padded across polished beams as he had glanced at his watch, poured himself another generous measure, looked at his watch once more and then decided at quarter

past one on a God-awful Saturday morning that he needed to call a COBRA meeting.
That had all been half an hour ago now.

“I want to know everything you know.”

Robert Harris rubbed the side of his skull, pads of his fingers concentrating on the temple, massaging, looking sternly across the twelve-man table at the three men seated opposite. The pain over his eyes was horrendous – literally blinding – and he was beginning to feel a little nauseous. The Prime Minister had been plagued by migraines since childhood. He was still floored by one at least three times a year. With an unsteady hand, he uncapped a bottle of Evian and sipped from it, hoping the migraine wouldn’t be too severe. A tingling hand pushed through his thick brown hair. He looked directly into the slate-coloured eyes of the man sitting in front of him. “I want to know everything you know about a drug called TK-214.”

A haze of pale blue smoke wafted from the cigar clenched between the Lieutenant Colonel’s teeth. When he spoke, ash dropped onto the tabletop. “I’m afraid I’m not following you, Rob.” He inhaled hard on the cigar and raised his white eyebrows.
“Oh, come on!” The Prime Minister bashed his numbed fist off the table in frustration. The Lieutenant Colonel didn’t even blink. “Do you think I’m that naïve? Guess who I got a phone call off tonight.”

Lieutenant Colonel Shaun Paige of the Royal Marines shrugged his decorated shoulders. Smoke sieved from his nostrils like a dragon’s breath.
“Lorraine Fielding,” said the Prime Minister. He pushed himself from the table and paced the room, head down,

hands dipped in the pockets of his black silk dressing gown. Slippers scuffed the lush carpet. He wore a white vest over a plump belly, and black silk pyjama bottoms. "That name ringing any bells?"
"Editor of the Breakfast Tree newspaper," Lieutenant Paige answered. He scratched unnecessarily at his neatly trimmed goatee and watched the Prime Minister as intently as he would an Afghan informer. "What's that deceitful gash got to do with me and my infantry, Rob?"

"I was hoping you could tell me that, Lieutenant," the Prime Minister said. He paused momentarily beside the plasma screen where the President of America had just virally wished him good luck with the ongoing crisis. Afterglow from the monitor brightened the dark room.

"I don't know what you're talking about, Rob."

"She asked me about a pharmaceutical trial backed by our military."
"Mr Prime Minister," Chief of police Victor Edmonds cut in. "If I may be dreadfully bold here and interrupt, I believe I speak for the Lieutenant and Deputy Prime Minister when I say we haven't got a clue what you have been told. I mean, pharmaceutical trials backed by the military, Lorraine-bloody-Fielding, riots...it all sounds terribly conspiratorial."
"Yes, it does."

"Lorraine's a car wreck, Rob," Andrew Herron, Deputy Prime Minister, said with a barely stifled yawn. "She's a disgusting creature. And I genuinely mean that. Just look how close she came to ruining your career. That harlot would happily besmirch anybody in public power - especially you – to sell that rag of hers."

"Maybe somebody should run a story about her dependency on alcohol then," Victor Edmunds said.

Lieutenant Paige smiled. Smoke escaped from between nicotine airbrushed teeth.
The Prime Minister sighed wearily and folded his arms across his chest. Forty-seven years-old; married but childless, to the same woman he had first met in and shared a classroom with many years ago at college. The thought of Clara upstairs in bed, asleep, naked, his sticky seed oozing from between closed legs, made him long to be cuddled up beside her. The pain in his head intensified. He forced himself not be get distracted.

"Look, this is not a witch hunt. I am not accusing anybody of anything here, but, as I'm sure you'll understand, I have a responsibility to investigate a claim made by a member of my public and I intend to fully adhere to it."
"Nobody here is questioning your dedication or commitment to the public. We just don't know anything about this TK-214 drug and what, if any, effects it has on its patients. I have been trusted in a position of command within the ranks of the military for over a decade. I can assure you that no pharmaceutical trial has ever been carried out inside that time without your consent. I give you my word, Rob."
The Prime Minister nodded his head slowly. Numbed fingers rubbed at the base of his neck.

Thunder screamed overhead.

"If you don't mind my asking," said Victor Edmunds. "But how did Lorraine Fielding come upon such balderdash?"

"A porter at a hospital in London approached her with the story after the news of Dennison Asaria's death spread. Apparently, he said he had seen numerous incidents where the alleged drug was administered to newborn babies without the parents' knowledge. He claimed to have obtained evidence."
"That's preposterous!" Andrew Herron scoffed.

"But on a more serious issue," the Lieutenant Colonel overtook. "My platoons have been moved into the capital and are on stand-by. Further instructions are required."
Robert Harris quickly fired a glance towards Lieutenant Paige. "Dependency on the military to halt future disorder has to be our last resort, Shaun. We have already discussed this in fine detail. Like I said last night – and I haven't changed my mind – there will be both political and practical difficulties having armed personnel policing the public. Tempers are already rife. The last thing I need to be dealing with right now is the equivalent of another Bloody Sunday."
"With all respect, Rob, these selfish scavengers need to be reminded that our – no, their – Armed Forces have paid the ultimate sacrifice to keep this country a safe place to live."

"And they will be, Lieutenant. Your men's services will be called upon, but only when and if it is categorically compulsory. We don't want to be premature putting boots on ground. The entire thing could just die down."
"It's not going to just die down though, is it?"

"Lieutenant," the Deputy Prime Minister hissed.

Wary glances were exchanged.

Robert Harris was quick to pick up on it. “Gentlemen, why do I get the impression you’re withholding information from me?”

A rap of knuckles against the door interrupted the briefing.

Rob bellowed for it to be opened and his PA apologised for disturbing the consultation, explaining that Lorraine Fielding was on the phone on hold.
“Line one?”

“Yes, sir,” his Private Assistant replied. “I told her you were sleeping, but she insisted. I thought it best to put her through.”
“You did the right thing. Thanks, Selene.”

He stormed over to the phone and snatched up the receiver.
“Lorraine?”

There was the briefest of delays.

“Mr Prime Minister.”

“Not going to lie to you, Lorraine, I’m not at all happy to be disturbed at such a late hour.”

“You’ve got bigger fish to fry than getting your beauty sleep.”
“It would seem not, Lorraine.”

“Mr Prime Minister, have you thought anymore about our last conversation?”
“It appears I don’t need to. I have discussed your allegation with my constitution, yes, but no further

evidence to back up your claim has presented itself." He frowned across to Lieutenant Paige. "I have been assured by my congregation that no further investigation is required."
"You mean you're happy to brush my allegation under the carpet?"
"Brush what exactly, Lorraine? You have no concrete evidence for me to reconsider my decision."

"You've changed. You're not the same leader you were two years ago."
"A lot has changed since then."

"You know I can't just sit on this story, don't you?"

"What story, Lorraine? You don't have one. And I'm warning you right now, if you dare release a story without any hardcore evidence to substantiate your claim, if you cause more panic, more fear, if you print even one word today that does not collaborate with the truth, I will personally see to it that your tiny little tabloid kingdom comes crashing down."

"Rob, please, meet with me. I can show you—"

"No!" the Prime Minister barked. "I'm sorry, Lorraine, I really am, but widespread anarchy is destroying Britain tonight. That must and does take centre stage to your little government scandal." He thumbed down on the plunger, injecting a blatant dose of sarcasm into his tone.

"I am warning you, Mr Prime Minister; do not ignore me."
"This conversation is over."

He replaced the receiver back into the cradle with an audible ping.
"Okay, gentlemen," he said, sitting back down, "I want to know everything you people know about TK-214."

The Lieutenant Colonel sighed audibly. "We've already been through this."
"That's right. But we have a small problem. I have a press conference at eight o'clock this morning to discuss the actions required by both police and the public in the dealing of this disorder. And although I have seen no physical evidence to consider the mentioning of this mythical drug, I can't shake the feeling that you men are holding back on something. Call it gut instinct. And that does not mean Lorraine Fielding will not splash it all over the front pages of her newspaper. So, gentlemen, I will ask you again – what is TK-214?"

The Deputy Prime Minister cleared his throat, resting his jowly chin on one meaty fist. "In the interest of that despicable crow and the potential threat she poses to an already fragile nation, I feel it only beneficial to ask if you are educated at all in the subject of HDP?"

The Prime Minister looked blank. The expression was louder than words.
"Very well," Andrew Herron continued. "HDP – Human Depletion Project to give it its official title – is a military and government backed scheme to prevent the world from overpopulating."
All eyes in the room locked on Andrew Herron as though he were a heat-seeker.
"Did you know, Mr Prime Minister, that for humanity to continue substantially existing as it is at present, one third

of the planet's population must expire to prevent a drain on the planet's resources?"
"I have heard similar theories. I've never really given it much thought." He crossed his arms over his chest and placed his left foot to his right knee. "What does HDP have to do with our current crisis?"

Andrew nodded slowly. "To understand the seriousness of the situation, Mr Prime Minister, first you must appreciate and recognize the ecological and agricultural fibres of such a project. Human beings have far exceeded their sustainable population range on the planet. Earth is carrying an overloaded capacity. Soon, we will no longer be capable of functioning at the current rate."

"What are you talking about?"

"Mr Prime Minister, please," Shaun Paige pleaded. "It's vital you hear this." "Rob, may I be dreadfully bleak with you?" the Deputy Prime Minister asked. "One third of the human population needs to perish for civilization to continue. It's that simple. If the world's population should double – triple even – by the end of the century, the unpleasant outcome could very well lead to the complete extinction of humanity. Overpopulation is desperately spiralling out of control. Our resources are being consumed quicker than Earth can replenish them. There are currently seven billion people on the planet right now. That figure is expected to rise to nine or even ten billion over the next twenty years."

"There has to be an effective alternative," Victor Edmunds said flatly. "And thankfully there is."

"So how exactly does TK-214 fit into this?"

"We cannot, nor do, condone mass genocide. Not statistically speaking anyway. So we are left with no other option than creating scenarios where mass depopulation is the only operational applicant."

"You mean you're murdering people."

"No. We are preserving a future."

"Why wasn't I told of this?"

"It was deemed classified."

"Deemed classified by who?"

"Mr Prime Minister, if you pause and take—"

"Deemed classified by who?"

"I'm afraid I'm not at liberty to divulge that information."

The Prime Minister shook his head slowly.

"I understand this might come as a shock, but please try to—"
"What does it do?"

"Mr Prime Minister, please try and understand that I am not permitted—"
"I want to know what that drug does. And I want to know right now. If you truly are orchestrating the demise of innocent people and depopulating the planet then I want to know exactly what TK-214 actually does. Does it make

them ill? Give them some kind of super flu?"

"No. It does none of those."

"Then how does it depopulate Earth?"

"It creates an infection."

"What kind of infection?"

"I am not at liberty to say."

The Prime Minister jumped up and grabbed the leather chair by its armrest, spinning it, hauling it up off the floor, roaring with betrayal and launching the swivel chair against the wall. A monsoon of faux leather, plastic, metal, and castors poured onto the carpeted floor. Rain pelted a rhythmical soundtrack from outside. It sounded like somebody rattling a giant maraca.

"I want answers!" he bellowed, breathlessly. "And I want them right now!"
"I'm afraid I am in no position to give them to you."

"Then who is?"

"That would be me."

The fifth voice – one Robert Harris immediately recognized but didn't quite believe – boldly echoed throughout the briefing room. This newcomer strode purposefully from the congealing shadows at the bottom of the room. There was an access point down there, but he hadn't heard the door open at any point during the COBRA meeting.

Which means he was already in the room before the briefing had begun or had stealthily crept in at some point during; slipping unnoticed into the inky blackness of early morning.

Both possibilities sent a volley of shivers down the Prime Minister's spine.
The newcomer stepped up to the table, arms at his sides, wearing a naval ceremonial uniform complete with sapphire gloves. A compilation of glossy medals decorated the first-rate tunic. The Prime Minister – slightly embarrassed for having displayed his frayed temper under such noble scrutiny – stumbled awkwardly over the remains of the chair. The three other men quickly rose to their feet and saluted.
"Your Highness," Robert Harris breathed.

The Prince of Cambridge – son and heir to the King of England – stepped from the shadows. He respectfully saluted each man individually and turned his direct attention on Robert Harris. He nodded briefly.

"Rob, allow myself to apologise wholeheartedly for keeping you in the dark on this one."

"Your Highness, please help me to understand how something like this could be permitted."

The Prince nodded slowly.

"I believe we need to have a talk."

CHAPTER 17

Ethan Hardcastle closed and locked the front door, sprinting down the narrow hall and exploding into his brother's front room. Dave was standing at the window, peeping around the lace curtain, squinting down into the communal gardens of the complex. It seemed quiet down there for the time being.

"Mummy, I feel sick," Lincoln groaned. He tugged irritably on the sleeve of Karris's coat. Karris Hardcastle stooped in front of him and placed the back of her hand against his flushed forehead. He did feel a little clammy, but with everything that was going on, it was only to be expected. Ethan manoeuvred around the La-z-Boy recliner, past the 50" LCD TV with its wizardry cinema system. He ran envious eyes over the laptop sitting proudly on the desk in the corner. A copious heap of DVD's and Blu-Rays were stacked like Lego bricks beside it.
Shit, those arseholes would've had a field day if they'd got in here!
He stepped up beside Dave.

"How are the ribs?"

"Okay," Ethan answered. Truth be told, they stung like a bitch. "They're a little bruised, but I'll be fine. How's it looking out there?"
He dreaded the answer.

"It seems quiet for the moment."

"We should probably think about moving on."

Dave nodded, but didn't turn away from the window.

The persistent whine of the air raid siren was subtly quieter now every door and window in the flat was closed, but makes no mistake, it was there. Like a song stuck in your head that you're not able to identify, humming along despite not knowing the words, wishing that bloody beat would just disappear...

"Hey, honey-bear, you're a little hot, but I'm sure it's nothing to worry about." She took Lincoln by the hand and led the boy towards his father.

"Hey, champ," Ethan said, feigning happiness. "Why don't we see if we can find some cartoons on Uncle Dave's TV?"

"I'm sorry, little man, but you'll have to watch it in the bedroom. There's a DVD player in there." Dave moved away from the window and nodded towards a closed door opposite. "Marcel sometimes stays at weekends. He's got all kinds of cartoons in there. I think there's even a few Scooby Doo."

"Marcel?" Ethan asked.

"Stefan's little boy."

Ethan ran a hand through his hair, sighing through his nostrils.

"Why can't he watch the TV in here?" Karris asked. She pointed towards the gargantuan resort of entertainment behind him.

From the lobby, the fountain blasted an explosion of frothy pink spittle three-storeys high.

"Because, there's something on the TV that you need to see, but he doesn't."

"If you mean the death of Prince Jasper then you're too late. We already know about it. It's truly awful."

"It is. I don't even know how they managed to break into the Palace."
"I guess tonight's the night for peculiar occurrences."

"Don't blame yourself for what happened out there. You had no choice."
Ethan was desperate to put the carriage of guilt onto another track; divert it from its current destination – his aching heart – derail the fucker if he had no other choice. He resorted to drastic tactics.

"I thought you and Stefan broke up."

"We're taking things slowly."

"You are?"

"We're just seeing where things are going."

"I take it his wife knows about you now?"

Dave shrugged his shoulders. He looked more than a little embarrassed.
Ethan laughed humourlessly, mockingly.

"It is what it is," Dave said quietly, eyes glittery.

"Is he still hitting you?"

"What? No, of course he isn't. And I told you last time it was partially my own fault."

“Come on! You’re better than that!”

“He’s harmless. Honestly.”

“He will be if he touches you again.”

A sheet of silence blanketed both men.

From the bedroom, Ethan could hear the strained voice of Shaggy talking to his old friend, old pal, old dear, dear buddy, Scoob’s.
“What’s this thing you want to show me then?” Ethan eventually asked. He crossed the room and picked up the remote control from the coffee table. He turned the goliath on. The room flashed from pitch black to deep blue.

“There’s nothing on there,” Dave said. He sat down on the swivel chair in front of the laptop. “The TV stopped broadcasting half an hour ago. You need to see what’s on here.”

Ethan wasn’t listening. Instead, he was staring in disbelief, mouth wide open, catching flies as his mother would say, captivated by the bright blue screen and the white words scrolling across it. He heard Dave turn the laptop on. He heard it buzz into life, heard rain pelting the window, and heard the familiar ding ding ding dung as the Windows logo appeared. He heard it all, but he saw none of it. Ethan Hardcastle refused to turn away from that TV.

THIS IS A PUBLIC SERVICE ANNOUNCEMENT

PLEASE REMAIN CALM

ALL SCHEDULED BROADCASTING HAS BEEN CANCELLED
PLEASE DO NOT PANIC

RIOTING REPORTED IN EVERY MAJOR CITY IN BRITAIN
BUCKINGHAM PALACE HAS BEEN ATTACKED

PRINCE JASPER CONFIRMED DEAD

ARMED FORCES ARE NOW TO ASSIST POLICE

DENNISON ASARIA BODY HAS BEEN RELEASED

THE CAUSE OF HIS DEATH:BRAIN ANEURISM

"What the—"

Dave waved him quiet.

"It's about to start. It's on loop."

"What is?"

"Ladies and gentlemen," a strongly authoritative voice boomed from the surround-sound speakers. The solid tone commanded attention. Ethan figured that was why he had been used.
What kind of fucking job is that?

"As I am sure you're aware by now, widespread rioting is unfurling across England today with chaotic scenes having now been confirmed in every major city in Britain. Thousands of yobs took to the streets through the night to demonstrate against the death of a local black man named Dennison Asaria. Unfortunately, Mr Asaria died yesterday morning in police custody. Immediately, police brutality was presumed. A post-mortem has since been conducted with the full sanctioning of Mr Asaria's mother, and I can now inform you that Dennison died of a brain aneurism, His death – regrettable as it is – was inevitable. The police are not to be held accountable. Unfortunately, with a current death toll standing around 800 it is far too late for some poor people. Buckingham Palace has been attacked. Prince Jasper and his fiancée Adela were beaten. It is my solemn duty to inform you that the Prince has since died from his injuries at the Angel of Forgiveness hospital. The King and other Royal constituents have been flown to a more secure location, but we believe they were present during the attack."

There was a sound from the bedroom. Ethan looked away from the TV for the first time and saw Karris open the door. His wife was holding a wastepaper bucket under her arm and, for no apparent reason, déjà vu struck, catapulted him back to his driveway yesterday, watching her step onto the porch with a bowl of salad under her arm. Had it only been yesterday? It felt like a millennium had passed.

"I'm so sorry," she whispered. "Lincoln's been sick. He got some of it on Marcel's quilt."

"Is he okay?" asked Ethan.

"Yes. I think he's just frightened."

"Aren't we all?" said Dave.

"Do you mind if I fetch him a glass of water?"

"No, don't be silly. There are bottles in the fridge."

"I will wash Marcel's quilt for you."

"Don't worry about it. Thankfully he's in Scotland with Stefan at the moment."
Ethan turned back to the TV.

"Since the death of Prince Jasper – and to some degree in retaliation of it – all police have now been removed from the streets. Armed Forces have been granted permission from the Prime Minister to enforce the law with a first-ever country-wide curfew. Between now and six A.M. any person found on the streets will be greeted with an insensitive and certified approach. Please, return to your homes; encourage loved ones you know to be out and about inside. This is your only warning. Anyone found on the streets after this announcement will be categorically dealt with."
"Dealt with?" Ethan mumbled. "I don't like the sound of that much."
"Me neither."

The screen faded to black for a few seconds, flashing blue when the public service announcement rolled onto the screen again. Ethan realised it was playing on loop and pressed the stand-by button, ending the broadcast. He dropped the remote control onto the recliner. The realization of how severe the situation had become suddenly grasped him with the surprise and fear of a spider's fang penetrating a big toe in the dead of night.

"You need to see this," Dave said. He was leaning over his laptop, the soldiers on his left expertly tapping away on the keyboard. "Internet's a bit shaky, but I've still got a connection."

"What is it?" Ethan asked.

"A video," answered Dave. Fingertips click-clacked a few more keys. "It was uploaded onto YouTube an hour ago."

Ethan groaned loudly. "Do I really want to see it?"

"I think you probably need to."

The laptop buzzed as the opening page of the video-sharing network fired up. There was a brilliant white screen. And then the usual logo and emoticons appeared on the left side. Below, where the recommended videos usually were, there was a variety of blocked images, all parading the same hooded youth pointing a gun at an older man wearing a suit. The blog descriptions below ranged from BRITISH RIOTS to HOODED CHAV DECLARES WAR.
"What is this?" Ethan demanded to know.

"Just watch it," Dave said. He pressed the ENTER key and a pictorial egg timer flashed on the screen. "This should explain things a little clearer."Ethan sat down on the arm of the recliner and waited for the video to load.

A painfully long second passed.

Ethan looked nervously around the apartment.

Then the video began to play.

The drenched man in the footage was in his mid-forties, colossally overweight, wearing a black two-piece suit; pale yellow shirt, green tie, and Wellingtons. His neatly cropped hair was matted to his skull. It seeped down into a great bushy beard, giving him the impression of a rabbi. Small, round, rain-splattered glasses sat proudly on his nose. He had a microphone gripped firmly in one hand. At first, Ethan mistook him for another bloody journalist, but then he spoke, introducing himself as the Mayor of London, and Ethan stood corrected.

Why the hell is he standing on the banks of the Thames?

There was only the Mayor on film for the moment, but behind him – on the opposite side of that slow-flowing river of pollution Parliament and its money-orientated litter were so proud of – black storm clouds were exposed by hundreds of burning fires. The stretching flames looked Fisher Price plastic from that distance.
"Hello, I am the Mayor of London, Kenny McKay, and I am here on the banks of the Thames at," he quickly glanced at the illuminated face of his watch, "two-thirty on a dreadful Saturday morning." He held up his hands at this point to express how bad the rain actually was, "to speak with a young participant of the violent disorder destroying the country. I have stressed that under no point during this interview will the youngster be apprehended for his contribution to the anarchy. I have given him my word." A youth crunched his way across the pebble beach and stopped beside the Mayor. He wore a grey hooded top with the drawstring pulled so tight only rock star sunglasses concealing his eyes were visible. A scarf was wrapped like the bandages of a Mummy around the lower

part of his face. He stood alone; arrogant, obnoxious, flashy, and there wasn't a breath of fear in his body. His Parker duffle coat was wringing wet. A barefaced indication of how long he'd been looting.
"The Britain we know and love died tonight in an orgy of murder and mindless violence that has continued now for nearly twenty-four hours, and shows no sign of relenting. Here is Darrell, who has agreed to meet with me to shed some light on the frightening state of affairs occurring in that burning city behind me. London: once noble, dignified, proud, the beaming capital of Britain, but tonight – following the death of Dennison Asaria – it has been turned into a burning, bloody island of lawless barbarity. In your own words please describe what this protest means to you?"
The youth looked gloatingly over his shoulder and then glared right back into the camera. Ethan could swear those eyes beneath the sunglasses were smirking. "Well, you see, fat man," Darrell throatily chuckled. "London is a city of two worlds. You understand that? One half has well-educated, well-paid, pretty boys and girls living in £900 a month apartments. And then you've got the other half, where people like me – unemployed, crashing in a hostel, living out of fucking black bags—"

"Please refrain from using sewer language on air—"

"Shut up, fat man! Do you want to hear this or not?"

Kenny McKay nodded and raised the microphone towards Darrell's cloaked mouth again.

"I have a nine year-old brother, yeah, and you know something; there're parts of this city – your city – that he ain't or won't ever see. I mean, yeah, he's heard of Big

Ben, the Houses of Parliament, the London Eye, but they're all foreign landscapes to him. He can't afford the bus money out of Peckham. I have friends who can't even leave their estate for fear of being shot."

"And what does leading an underprivileged life have to do with the death of Dennison Asaria?"

"Absolutely nothing," Darrell confirmed. "Kid's dead. So what? There ain't anything I can do about it. Just because some brother dies in a police cell doesn't mean I'm going to start tearing London up. I'm as sure as hell not protesting."

"Then why are you doing it?"

"I'm making a declaration."

"What declaration?"

"A declaration of war," Darrell growled into the microphone. "I have a message for your fearless leader, Robert Harris, Mr Prime Minister, as you prepare to send your brave men into my world: surely even a pompous millionaire of a millionaire can see there will only be one outcome. Your world will fall beneath the rise of my crusaders. My people are brave. Their time has come. They will stand up and be counted. For centuries, you, Mr Prime Minister, have looked down on my people; regarded them as worthless deadbeats. You believe it to be okay to treat my people with no respect. You think they will never accomplish anything. But you're wrong. My people have brought those two worlds – yours and mine – together. Now we're tearing the fucker up. My people are strong. My people are warriors."

"Your people are setting fires and stealing computer games,"
"I think we'd better wrap it up there," the cameraman said off film.
"Mr Prime Minister," Darrell continued, masked face filling the lens. "I implore you to bring your Armed Forces into my world. They are like you – old, fat, soft. My people will rip their yellow fucking hearts out. We will not cower to your threatening tactics. We will not surrender. We will not forgive. We will not stop until every last one of your disgusting people has been wiped from the face of the Earth." Darrell paused and snapped his hooded head towards the Mayor. "Starting with you,"

The camera picked up the muffled pleas of Kenny and his faithful cameraman, and then, suddenly, an explosion shattered the stillness. The Mayor was thrown – arms outstretched, head pouring blood – crashing into the icy depths of the Thames.
"No!" Ethan screamed, "Lord, no!"

There was a brief glimpse of a smoking handgun; black heavens, more pleading, rolling thunderheads, shingle, the cameraman's feet, and then the focus turned into the cheapest found-footage film ever, recording shaky, motion-sickness inducing footage as the cameraman ran for his life across the beach. Another sharp retort and the camera fell to the floor.
"My God," Ethan breathed. "They've murdered the Mayor."
"On live TV, too."

"We need to get out of here. We need to get Mum and Lee and then get out of this country."

"And go where?"

Ethan shrugged his shoulders. "I don't care as long as we're far enough from Britain. Maybe someplace where it's hot; where there's a beach; somewhere somebody's not trying to rip my fucking head off every five seconds."

"But how do we get there?"

"What do you mean?"

"Airports are on lockdown."

"They are?"

"Ethan, have you not been paying attention to anything tonight?"

"No, Dave." Ethan compressed the syllables between clenched teeth. "I have been too busy watching Harold get kicked to death."

"Okay, okay, you're right, I'm sorry. I'm just a little rattled."

"It's not important. What is important is what we do next."

"Like I said," Dave mumbled, turning the laptop off and pushing the monitor down. "The airports are on lockdown. They have armed soldiers refusing to allow anybody in or out of the country. The ferry ports are under quarantine, too."

"Tell you the truth, mate; we're going to have our work cut out just trying to get back to my house. I've been out there already. It's like hell on Earth."

"Where's your truck?"

“The little bloody bastards overturned it when I reached the city. We barely made it here in one piece.”

“There is perhaps one way.”

“I’m listening.”

“Stefan drives a taxi. It’s parked around the back. He has to work weekends so he can claim income support. If it’s still in one piece – and I have no reason to believe otherwise – then we could use it to get to yours.” Ethan nodded his head. “I never thought I’d be thanking Stefan.”

“He’s a good man, Ethan.”

“I’m sure Darrell’s father would have said the same thing about him this time yesterday.”

A brief pause was inducted into the fast-flowing conversation. The air raid siren continued to screech its cautionary prophecy of damnation, punishment, abysmal penance from the netherworld. The whole thing seemed like a hellish nightmare. It reminded him of a film he and Karris had watched a couple of weeks ago on Netflix; a Guillermo Del Toro movie based on a book about society being rocked by a sudden increase in the number of violent assaults on individuals. It was a popcorn movie (nowhere near as good as the book Karris had said), but there was one scene where the main character was trapped inside his home as his neighbour went on a murderous rampage. Boulders of fear tumbled down his spine.

Thunder roared like a rabid animal caught in a bear trap.

Karris opened the bedroom door and stepped into the front room. She was carrying Lincoln once again in her arms. His eyes were red-rimmed and his skin was frightfully pale.

"Here comes trouble," joked Ethan. He hoped humour really was the best form of medicine. He fretfully crossed the room. "Are you feeling okay, champ?"
"No," Lincoln complained.

"No? What's wrong, buddy?"

"He's burning up. And he's been sick again," Karris answered.
"Are you not feeling well, mate?" He stroked the side of his son's flushed face. "We will get you feeling better soon, I promise."
"I feel sick, Daddy."

"You do? Just hang in there. We're going home in a second or two."
"Will they still be there?"

Ethan paused and held his breath. He knew who "they" were, but pretended he didn't have a clue. Ignorance sometimes truly is bliss. "Will who still be there?"
"The bad men,"

Ethan choked back a sob. The corner of his eye revealed Karris turning her back on her husband and son. Even the hammering rain couldn't conceal her crying.
"Look, honey-bear; I am your Daddy and I give you my word that you're safe. I'm not going to let anybody hurt you. I love you. And I always will. There's nothing to be

scared about. I will make sure there are no bad men at home."
"Let's go," said Dave.

Ethan nodded and grabbed a hold of his son's hand.

CHAPTER 18

The Prince smiled patiently and stood in front of the briefing table. Lieutenant Paige, along with the Chief of Police and the Deputy Prime Minister, were excused and dismissed to their required locations. The Prince had warned the coming hours would be incredibly bleak and busy for everybody. He shook each man's hand, wishing them the best of luck, thanking them individually for their alliance to his father's regime. To Robert, it seemed more like farewell bidding than appreciative recognition. The Prime Minister sat at the table, eyes closed, fireworks display erupting behind closed lids, head aching, fingers on his left hand completely numb, listening to rain beating the above. Once they were on their own, the Prince removed his peaked visor hat and placed it on the table.

"I want to apologise once again for keeping this from you, Rob. It was not the correct procedure, but my hands were tied."
"Why was I not notified about TK-214, you're Majesty?"

The Prince sighed loudly. "It was my father's decision. He believed – as do I – that you had enough on your plate already."
The Prime Minister shook his head. "All due respect, your Highness, but I am the leader of the United Kingdom. It is part of my job description to have a lot on my plate."

"Look, you're taking this personally. There's really no need. You had a lot going on. You didn't need the added pressure of a pharmaceutical trial that may or may not have been successful. There was the ongoing conflict in Afghanistan; the Tuberculosis outbreak in Devon, not to

mention your private life having already been dragged through the public-wringer."
"I take full responsibility for mine and Lorraine's affair."

"That's not important."

"As Prime Minister, I had a right to know."

"For Christ's sake, we're getting nowhere!" the Prince bellowed. Palm slapped table. "We are in the shit. I mean up to our necks in it." He took a breath and regained his composure. "Now, I believe the Deputy Prime Minister has already given you a detailed description of the why, what's, and how's."
Robert Harris nodded his pounding head.

"Then drop it," the Prince ordered.

The Prime Minister had a hundred more questions – vital questions – balancing precariously on the tip of his tongue, but the bass in the Prince's voice suggested he allowed his curiosity to fester. He gulped noisily from a bottle of water instead and waited compliantly for his superior to speak.
The King's first son brushed a speck of dust from the sleeve of his pristine tunic. When he next spoke, he refused point-blank to make eye contact with the Prime Minister.

"What I am about to tell you does not leave this room. Not a single monosyllable."
Robert Harris wanted to tell the Prince he had nothing to worry about, that he had sworn faithful allegiance to his father's every command, but his tongue was weighted, carpeting the bottom of his mouth, refusing to budge.

Robert realized it was paralysed with fear.

"We designed TK-214 back in '92. It was developed the following year with the intention of being an authentic weapon in reducing the earth's crowded population. The drug is a liquid solution, totally odourless, and is usually inoculated into selected babies at birth." The Prince paused for a moment and allowed that last part to fully absorb. "We choose newborns. It is far easier to administer without questions from overprotective parents."

The Prime Minister looked physically sick, but remained silent. He was determined to learn as much about this drug as possible.

The Prince seemed taken aback, but continued all the same. "The plan was fairly basic. We would instruct a trusted source to inject the selected babies after birth and allow the drug to remain dormant until puberty was reached. At this point some cataclysmic trigger would be pulled and the administration awakened, resulting in what has been happening in every major city in Britain tonight."

"Which is what, exactly?" the Prime Minister finally asked.

The Prince smiled charmingly. "A solidified circle of young people – black, white, Asian – launching a coordinated attack against society. You take away their job opportunities, their benefits, their prospects, their children, and they will retaliate by attacking our way of life."

"But what does all of this achieve?"

"You disappoint me, Rob, you really do," the Prince said. He stepped back from the table and paced the room, arms behind back, head down. "Do you remember the civil

unrest in London a few years back? Do you remember the riots? Do you remember those youths switching from looting to arson to murder in a window of only a few days? Do you remember the public crying out for Armed Forces to patrol the streets? You even chaired a discussion in Parliament about arming police officers. Do you remember? Now let me tell you what I remember. I remember people dying. I remember trouble knocking at peoples' front doors and those terrified civilians pleading for the government to resort to whatever measures were needed to stop the disorder. They wanted the rioters dead back then. They didn't care how it happened. They just wanted the violence to end. They sanctioned us; permitted, allowed us to open fire on the hordes. But we didn't. We held off. And the population has swelled in the meantime."
"Your Majesty, are you saying those rioters were contaminated by TK-214?"
The Prince swatted the question aside. "This time it was different. This time the main objective from the very beginning was to inflate the number of candidates and allow the destruction to peak."

"Let me get this straight," the Prime Minister said. "You are certifying for newborn babies to be injected with a fluid that will eventually turn them into feral teenagers, so you can gain public permission to execute them. All so the planet can reduce its crammed population. Is that right?"

"That pretty much describes the situation, yes."

"Forgive me, your Highness; but I'm failing to see how the authorised disposal of these candidates is capable of bringing the Earth's population back down to a habitable extent. Surely we're only scratching the surface."

"Statistically speaking, yes, you're absolutely right," the Prince answered. "But you're not taking into account the other prearranged occurrences mushrooming the planet on a yearly basis."
"Prearranged occurrences?"

"Cancer's the main one. But everything from epidemics in poverty-stricken countries to the endless war in the Middle East is regularly decreasing the population. Add a splash of austerity, financial aiding to terrorism, drone strikes, recessions, even bush fires in Australia; they all play a vital part in the cataloguing of the planet. We even get lucky every once in a while and Mother Nature vents her fury."
"Are you saying that cancer is man-made?"

The Prince looked uncomfortably down at his highly-polished shoes. "There are more imperative matters to discuss right now."
"My mother—"

"Rob," the Prince cut in. "I know. I am sorry. There is a cure. And we will release it." He licked his thin lips anxiously. "But only when the time is right."
"When the time is..." He cackled humourlessly. "I don't believe this. I don't believe it." He felt like he was a priest; hunched over, sitting in his little confessional booth, face pressed against the screen, listening to the disgusting sins of Adolf Hitler. He felt faint. He was certain he was about to pass out and he closed his eyes to regain composure. When he did, the image of his mother's wicker coffin tormented his brain.
"Rob, does the name Audra Alexi mean anything to you?"

“No,” the Prime Minister snapped. “Should it?”

“Not really. Audra is a highly classified case.”

Robert Harris raised his eyebrows.

The Prince overlooked his sarcasm. “Audra was a fifteen-year-old Lithuanian girl living in the East End of London. Two weeks ago, she died at the hands of her father. He strangled her to death.”

“Good Lord,” the Prime Minister said. His eyes widened. His aching brain was barely capable of soaking up any more distressing news.
“It sickens me to tell you this, but Audra murdered her twelve-day-old brother while her mother was asleep on the sofa. Her father had been at work and when he returned home he discovered his daughter had cooked his son for five minutes in the microwave.”

That’s it! My brain can’t take any more! It’s going into fucking meltdown!
The Prince allowed the horrific information to sink in. He watched the colour drain from the Prime Minister’s face. “The father – uncontrollable, distraught, and panicking – strangled Audra in a fit of rage. Personally, I don’t believe he intended to kill her, but the stench alone would have driven him into frenzy. Crushed her larynx, and she died right then and there. The son was dead, of course, burnt to a crisp. His poor mother received third degree burns to her hands trying to retrieve him. My wife cried for two entire hours after I finally told her what had required those three straight brandies. I haven’t drunk in years.”

"Why are you telling me this?"

"You said you wanted to know everything."

"Not this!" The Prime Minister roared. "I didn't want to know this!"

"Well, I'm afraid you have to. You see, Audra's corpse underwent an autopsy to see if drugs or alcohol had played any part in her psychotic eruption. The coroner found none. He also tested her for TK-214 and found no traces of the drug in her bloodstream. When her brother's poor body – what was left of it – was examined, however, the results detected fantastically minuscule remnants. The brother was a positive candidate."

"Audra's brother had been injected with TK-214?"

"That is what we believe, yes. Further inspection of Audra's major organs – the heart, the lungs, the liver, and the kidneys – began to reveal microscopic residue of TK-214 after her death. Tiny at first, it began to increase steadily by the hour; growing like moss on a rock despite the cadaver being blatantly deceased. We strongly believe this display of psychosis by Audra was the direct result of her baby brother being administered TK-214 shortly after birth. Which would also lead us to believe that our financially backed pharmaceutical trial – a trial created to manipulate the population of Earth – has evolved and adapted."

"Meaning what exactly, your Highness?"

"That we – man – are no longer the sole supplier of this medication. Perhaps the Alexi children – one positive, one negative – are to blame. Maybe they're not. We simply don't know. But another way has been found for TK-214 to spread. And spreading it is. We are looking into the possibility of it being airborne, but right now, we know very little apart from it is spiralling out of control, existing in previously unselected candidates. It is responsible for the anarchy we are seeing tonight. The death of my cousin, Jasper, is all the proof I need."

The Prime Minister tried to swallow, but his tongue was as dry as the Aral Seabed. "We currently have nearly three thousand arrested youths in police custody up and down the country. London is obviously worst hit. We are conducting blood tests on each prisoner and looking for any indication of either administered or flourishing TK-214 residue. So far, all have proved positive. The clean-up stage of this operation has begun. I have my soldiers in position. They will be going into action in the next twenty minutes."
"I told Shaun that I don't want boots on the ground."

"I know. I had no other choice but to overrule your command. Sorry Rob."
"So what now?" the Prime Minister asked. "I mean what's the worst case scenario here?"

The prince was reluctant to answer.

Thunder bellowed prehistorically.

"Worst case scenario? Do you really want to know?"

Robert Harris nodded slowly. But he didn't' think he did.

"We could be looking at every child in Britain – between the age of four and twenty – becoming maniacal, murdering monsters."

CHAPTER 19

They left Dave's flat together and descended the dark stairwell, the shriek of the air raid siren still beating their ear drums. Ethan had armed himself with a hammer from beneath the kitchen sink, refusing to defend himself with the sharp offerings of the knife drawer. Dave had removed the head of a broom and sharpened its handle, creating an improvised spear. The point wasn't too sharp, but it was better than nothing. They paid no attention to the blood-smeared fountain or its new gory attraction, and stepped outside where their ears and noses were assaulted once more. Ethan pulled Dave aside.

"Where's the taxi?"

Nervously, Ethan Hardcastle glanced around. The communal gardens circling the complex were deserted. There was a strip of Astroturf beneath a wooden jungle gym to his right, a patchwork of gravelly weeds to his left, and a yolk-yellow Citroen Picasso parked directly in front of him.
So where was Stefan's taxi?

It was pouring down; raining cats and dogs as they say, and the wind howled like a fanatically obsessed groupie from the Beatlemania years.
"Parked round the back," Dave shouted over the sizzling rain. "Couple of kids tried stealing it a few months back. Stefan parks it beneath the bedroom window so he could keep an eye on it."

"Kids, eh?" Ethan smiled. The irony of the situation was not lost on Dave. "Do you want to drive or should I?"

"You'll have to. I've left my glasses in the bathroom. The roads will be crammed."

"You stopped wearing contacts?"

"Stefan prefers me to wear glasses."

"Does he prefer you to wear a dress as well?"

"Ethan," Karris was quick to rebuke. "Now is not the time."

"Yeah, you're right," Ethan said. He accepted the car keys from his older brother and stepped into the downpour. "Stay here. I'll be back in five seconds."

True to his word, five seconds later and the distinctive clatter of a black cab chugged around the corner. Ethan pulled over in front of Karris and Lincoln, rolling his window down into the rubber groove. "Aye up pet," he boomed in his best cockney impersonation. "Need a Sherbet Dab get you down the ole' Joe Brown?"

Lincoln laughed as though his ribs were being prickled by the extraordinarily long arms of Mr. Tickle. It felt good to hear his son laugh like that; warmed his heart. Ethan honked the horn twice, no longer caring about the ravenous hordes.

"What did Daddy say, Mummy?"

"I really don't know honey-bear."

They all laughed.

Ethan grinned from ear-to-ear and tried to look mock-insulted. He opened his mouth to say something, but then Dave snatched open the opposite door and clambered inside, ordering Karris and Lincoln to do the same.

“What’s wrong?” Ethan demanded.

“We need to get moving.”

Ethan could tell something had spooked Dave, but he didn’t want to say what in front of Lincoln. Instead of prolonging their escape, Ethan revved the engine and looked into the rear-view mirror. The reflection made his heart scream like a famished Yeti. A dozen or so silhouetted shapes had materialized from the back of the complex and were walking towards the purring taxi; shouting, pointing, threatening, cursing. Somebody ran in front of the crawling cab and tried climbing onto the bonnet but Ethan acted quickly, reversing speedily, throwing the lout painfully to one side. He then turned the wheel crazily, as though his windswept eyes had just spotted an approaching iceberg in the North Atlantic Ocean. Two hooligans bounced a wheelie bin directly in his path (more of a blockage than a battering-ram) and Ethan had to slam on the brakes before he managed to gain any real momentum. The bin overturned, spilling garbage, and somebody kicked the passenger door heftily. Through the rain-spattered windscreen, Ethan watched a tidal wave of skin-tight jeans, bomber jackets, Doctor Marten boots, cargo pants, braces, and Ben Sherman shirts wash in front of his headlights. You didn’t need to be Einstein to work out why they were so pissed.

“They’re skinheads,” Dave said from the back.

“I know. The bastard must have put a call through to his cronies.”

Lincoln was screaming, yelling at the horde to leave his mummy and daddy alone. Ethan eased down on the clutch, pressed on the gas, feeling the bite, quickly

manoeuvring the taxi around the wheelie bin. A chunk of concrete dented the passenger door. Something shattered against the roof...again and again and again.
"Please tell me they're not petrol bombing us," Ethan groaned.
Somebody tried leaping on the bonnet once more, but only succeeded in breaking their jaw against the windscreen. One of the headlamps was kicked out. A wing mirror was destroyed.

"No," Dave answered. He was kneeling on the backseat and looking through the back window. "People in the complex are throwing glass bottles down."
"Shit, these people are your neighbours."

"I know. You've got to get us outta here!"

Chewing anxiously on his lower lip, Ethan Hardcastle eased down on the accelerator and began to pick up speed, roaring away from the chasing horde. The yellow retainer barrier was approaching at break-neck speed, choking their only escape route, but that wasn't his biggest problem. The gateway leading into the communal gardens had been forced open. Automatic locks and spearheaded railings had apparently been no match for fifty or sixty determined driving shoulders. Gates had buckled; and a constant stream of hooded degenerates were slipping through, climbing over railings mounted atop six foot high walls, jumping down, landing in soaking wet grass, charging towards the cab and its ransomed bounty.
"Fuck, Eth," Dave cursed. "We're blocked in."

"I know. Can we go back?"

Dave wiped condensation from the back window. It was too dark to see properly. Ethan swerved onto the grass verge and attempted a U-turn, but suddenly there was a regiment of skinheads kicking the driver's door. Clenched fists slammed against the windows. Karris screamed for him to do something.

What? What the hell can I do? Skinheads to the left of me, Hoods to the right, here I am – stuck in the middle with you!

"What are we going to do, Ethan?" Dave shouted. Ethan noticed his hands were gripped tightly around the makeshift spear. Ethan looked across to the hammer on the dashboard.

How many could we take out before they overpowered us?

"Daddy, I'm scared," Lincoln cried.

"You're okay, champ. You're going to be just fine."

Karris's eyes locked sternly on her husband's through the rear-view. Do something, those pale blue eyes commanded. Do something to save your family!

Ethan slapped his palm to his forehead. "Think, you useless fucker!"

A volcanic eruption of insanity exploded inside his brain. Cells finally woke up. Neurons clocked on. And before his suicidal idea could flourish fully, Ethan stomped both feet on the accelerator; boots slammed the pedal into floor, arms vibrating, metal cocoon bulleting down the path, almost spiralling out of control, head down, eyes squeezed shut, white stars dancing in front of irises. He swerved the car away from the drenched roadblock and onto the grass verge.

“I hope you know what you’re doing!”

“Keep down!”

“Why?”

“Just do it, Karris!”

He heard a rustling from the back of the taxi and glanced into the rear-view mirror. He saw the backseat was completely empty. They must be on the floor, wondering if he’d finally lost his mind. A hooded youth bounced off the bonnet, coiling over the roof, hitting the ground hard. Ethan didn’t even bother to look back.
Thunder bellowed. A flash of sheet lightning illuminated everything in crisp white. It bathed the horde at the gates in subtle shades of purplish blue. And in that moment – that dreadful moment – he noticed the eyes of the hooded legion had turned completely white. No irises. No colour, just the same milky whiteness of a ninety-year-old cataract sufferer. Ethan didn’t know if what he saw was a trick of the lightning or if his overworked brain had merely imagined the whole thing. And he wouldn’t get a chance to find out.

At that precise moment, the taxi sped uncontrollably up the grass verge, miraculously avoiding smashing into a fern, screaming like the Mad Hatter, knuckles white, head bouncing off the roof as car temporarily turned into plane and left the ground, wheels spinning, sailing through the air, bonnet crashing into railings, abolishing them, taking a huge chunk of the wall with it, crashing onto the other side, axles jarring, wheels hitting road but refusing to grip, nose cracking painfully against dashboard, and then he quickly regained control; taxi obediently flipping back under his command, refusing to tip on its side, coaxed back onto four wheels before roaring off into the darkness of early morning.

CHAPTER 20

It would have been quicker to drive straight through the town and follow the old viaduct back to the moors, but Ethan had already lost one vehicle to the rioting flock and, with the threat of armed soldiers patrolling the streets, he wanted to keep a safe distance between his family and the hot zone areas. He found a well-thumbed A-Z map in the glove compartment and passed it through the money-slot to Dave, who quickly got to work locating an escape route, following the thin red and blue lines with his finger, using the screen of his mobile for a weak light. Ethan floored the accelerator and fired them away from the chaotic scene at the complex.
"Where are we, Dave?" Ethan asked.

"I'm looking. Just give me a minute, yeah?"

"Hurry up!"

"Okay, I've found us. Right, you need to keep going straight and then take the first left at the Golden Phoenix restaurant. From there you take Barton Bridge over to Grove Lane. We can take the country lanes from there back to your house."
"What's Grove Lane?"

"I don't think we'll need to worry about rioting there."

"Why?"

"It's a private road. There's a cul-de-sac where the healthy and wealthy live."
"They sound like perfect victims to me."

Twenty minutes later and (perhaps for the first time in its elaborate history) the macadam covering Grove Lane was visited by the balding tyres of a black cab. Ethan allowed the vehicle to roll to a complete stop in the middle of the road, but kept the engine turning. He looked up at the row of detached town houses running along both sides of the smooth road. His envious eyes suddenly forgot about the rioting in town; momentarily put his mother and brother's safety on the backburner. He inhaled the wonderful view his one remaining headlight revealed. This leafy slice of desirability was what it was all about; the reason he got up each morning and worked his socks off, so that one day – one fucking day – he could give his wife and son a taste of the Good Life. The cars parked on the marble driveways ranged from Mercedes to BMW, and included even the occasional Lamborghini. And every front lawn was immaculately groomed.

This was what he had always wanted. This was what Karris deserved. He could see her now; collecting the morning paper, Bella tucked under one arm, and waving at the neighbourhood paperboy (would he be wearing a backwards baseball cap, baggy cargo shorts, and a basketball vest over bronzed arms and legs? Of course he would), paper-sack hanging low on hip, peddling through wonderland, Karris turning, almost colliding with a buffed-up version of himself, coffee flask under one arm, smiling gleaming pearls, striding towards the showroom BMW Pickup, complaining he was going to be late with the tone of a man whose bed made itself in the morning. This barrel-shaped dollop of land nestled amongst the crime and infidelity of the city was what he wanted – needed – to be a part of; keeping you to yourself, refusing the meddling public and their untrained dogs and litter-dropping, chocolate-smothered children access.

Jesus, you're even beginning to think like them!

Ethan turned in his seat, one arm resting on the wheel, and opened his mouth to speak when something crashed into the front passenger door with an almighty BANG! Instinctively, Ethan leapt to one side and, as he did, the passenger window exploded. A shower of sharp daggers drenched him. Nuggets of lethal shrapnel were flung on him and he was forced to raise his hands to protect his eyes. Karris cried out in either fear or pain from the back. Trembling fingers on his right hand reached for the wheel as the fingers on his left jiggered the gear stick into first. Screeching tyres rolled the vehicle forward before another explosion smashed into the back passenger door. "Fucking hell," Dave bellowed. "Some maniac is shooting at us!"

Ethan squinted in the direction the three shots had fired from, but he couldn't see anything. He could barely make out the outline of a town house to his left, but there were no lights on, no indication life existed behind those black windows.
"Why would somebody be shooting at us?" Karris blared.

"I don't know. Dave, can you see anything?"

"No, but the shooter must be close."

"All three bullets came from the left, yeah?"

"Yeah. Is the car okay?"

"It's still driveable, if that's what you mean. Stefan's going to need a new front window, though."

“Then get us out of here!”

Ethan nodded and sat upright. As he reached for the steering wheel again, he clearly heard the sound of a front door opening and heavy footfalls crunching gravel. His ears detected the screech of a gate opening; squeaky hinges, pouring rain, and then the sound of a gun being broken in half and reloaded. Ethan stepped on the accelerator and sped down the road. The explosive discharge gave chase.
The number plate was eradicated. The galloping cab was shoved further along the wet road, spinning, Ethan once again losing control, feet stepping on the brake despite his brain warning against it. The wheels locked and the tyres squealed, but the taxi kept going. The tyres were old, balder than Dave, failing to grip the soaking macadam. The car continued down the street with the speed of an express train. Ethan spun the wheel as though he was a DJ on an Ibiza beach during the summer festival.
“Look out!”

Ethan Hardcastle heard the warning, but didn’t see the black Range Rover until it was too late. He applied the handbrake, having no other option, and prayed to God that they wouldn’t flip. Feet stomped on the brake, hands cranked the steering wheel, seatbelt chomped into his neck, yet the black cab sailed disobediently across the road, screeching, squealing, a shower of sparks rushing off its side as it clashed briefly with the Range Rover, bumped onto the kerb, and crashed bonnet-first into a brick wall. Ethan’s head bounced off the leather steering wheel with all the sensitiveness of an emery board filing his foreskin. He winced and allowed his head to fall back against the headrest. A bulbous drop of blood pushed through the follicles of his eyebrow and slithered down the side of his face. The sound of the pouring rain hammering against the metal roof filled the taxi. It was all he could hear. It slalomed over the windscreen, made it impossible for him to see anything outside. Even if both headlights had been working, the curtain of rain wouldn't have revealed anything. All Ethan could see was the parked Range Rover and nothing more. And that was that.

"Everybody okay?" he slurred.

"No," Dave spluttered from the back. "I think I've shit myself.
"If you have then it'll be a fifty quid fine."

From the back of the taxi, on hands and knees, forehead resting against the same rubber runner that thousands of feet had trampled on throughout the years, where hundreds of inebriated passengers had spoiled themselves, Dave Hardcastle rose to his knees. He wasn't bleeding, he wasn't injured. Karris climbed onto the backseat, still clutching her terrified son in her arms. They looked frightened. They looked startled. But they weren't hurt. Dave flopped one of the spring seats down and crashed onto it. He massaged the base of his neck, wincing. "Why would somebody want to shoot us? We weren't causing any trouble."
"Are you okay?"

"A little whiplash,"

"I told you to wear your seatbelt." Fumbling fingers gripped the door handle and he shoved it open. "Lincoln okay?"
"Yeah, he's fine, aren't you, honey-bear?" Karris answered, stroking her son's ruffled hair. "Don't go out

there, Ethan. The shooter might still be in the street."

"I hope he is." Ethan whispered through clenched teeth. Fingers tightened around the hammer. Boots swapped steering panel for saturated pavement, and he slipped drunkenly from the taxi. Trembling hands reached for the sturdiness of that pillar of British society – the red post-box – to stop him sprawling on his backside.
Thank God I didn't smash into that!

Downstairs lights were on in the house whose front wall he'd just demolished. But nobody came out. Apparently nobody cared about the commotion. A soaking, loaded skip was in the gated driveway. Ethan could see two padlocks fastened to a bulky chain. In such an upmarket part of town, the tamper-proof gates looked as out of place as an orange hat in Greenville. Ethan could see three or four silhouettes at the window, peeping around lace curtains, and he raised his arms, the closest he could come to an apology.

"My Lord," Dave whispered, keeping his voice low. "What happened here?"
Ethan spun around at the sound of his brother's voice, ribs throbbing, head throbbing, and saw Dave standing on the opposite side of the cab. He was slack-jawed, staring disbelievingly at a lamppost on the opposite side of the road.
How could it have come to this? How could the government have allowed the violence to escalate into this? Ethan Hardcastle was no virgin to modern society. Like everybody else, he'd heard of the sickening stories about crimes on trains, in pubs, trams, takeaways, buses, shopping malls, all committed by the youth of today. He'd heard of organized gangs creating trouble, going to bullet-

blasting war with other gangs; he'd heard about postcode battles, but none of it had ever infringed on his life. Trouble had never come knocking at his front door. And that was the way he liked it. Society might well be in a blender, but it was not his fault. And it was up to the government to stop it from being switched on. Dennison Asaria hadn't been dead for twenty-four hours yet, but inside his fast-beating heart something told him this had nothing to do with the teenager's death anymore.
Darrell had been right.

This was war.

The kid was dead, of course. There was no doubt about that. He had been hung from the lamppost, hands tied behind his back, tongue protruding from bluish lips. The knot around his neck had been hastily tied, as if Jack Ketch had returned from the grave for one final execution. The sight of the youngster's purple, bloated face made Ethan wanted to vomit. He must have only been around eleven or twelve, had probably never even kissed a girl, and yet somebody had decided to murder this poor boy and leave his corpse hanging like some kind of prized pig. The poor kid had emptied his bowels as his final breath was slowly strangled from screaming lungs.
"Hey, what's that?" Dave said. He was pointing at the wringing wet boy.
Ethan took another step forward, now standing close enough that he could reach up and touch the trainers laced to the dead kid's feet. There was a piece of cardboard stapled to the front of the boy's coat. The overhead illumination from the lamp revealed the words NO LOOTERS in hastily scribbled marker pen.
"My Lord," Dave breathed. "The poor boy must have been terrified."

"Do you think our friend with the itchy trigger finger had anything to do with it?"
"He faced a fair trial," a voice boomed from behind the men. "The jury found the defendant unanimously guilty."

Ethan and Dave turned and saw an old man standing in the middle of the road. He was wearing a full-length riding coat buttoned over his tall frame; black Stetson proudly sitting atop pure silver hair, impeccably clean shaved. He appeared to be in either his late sixties or early seventies, but much more agile on his feet than their mother. Ethan's eyes dropped down to the double-barrel shotgun he was holding. Thunder bellowed from the black heavens.

"He was found guilty, you say?" Ethan placed the hammer on show, displaying it to the gunman. "What was his punishment?"
"I think you know the answer to your own question."

"You killed him?"

"He was found guilty,"

"And what was his crime, exactly?"

"Murder in the first degree,"

Ethan looked at Dave. Dave looked at Ethan. The muzzle of the shotgun was lowered slightly.

"Are you the prick that tried to shoot us?" Ethan roared over the windswept rain. He had only been outside for a few seconds, but already his hair was matted to his skull.
"I'm sorry about that."

"You're sorry? You almost blow my head off and you say sorry?"

"I saw your car pull over in the middle of the road. I thought you might have been friends or relatives of him," He poked the shotgun towards the dead boy. "I've been on watch most of the night. We had some trouble earlier."

"The whole country has had some form of trouble or another tonight. My stepfather was beaten to death by these scumbags. I don't know whether my mother, brother, and friend have suffered the same fate. But I'm not going around blowing peoples' fucking heads off."

"Eth, calm down," Dave warned.

"No, Dave, I won't calm down. And neither should you. He could have killed you tonight. He could have killed both of us."

"I'm truly sorry about opening fire. Really, I am. My name is Earl Topinka, and I live right there across the road." The old man took another step forward. The huge muzzle of the shotgun was now trained on the soaking wet floor, but that didn't stop Dave's bowels from liquefying. He looked up at the swaying corpse and scratched his smooth chin thoughtfully.

"What did he do?" Dave asked.

"My next door neighbour, an old lady called Mavis Ablinson, was sleeping tonight despite the rioting in town. My wife and I had been keeping a close eye on her; it's that type of neighbourhood, but around one o'clock this boy broke into her house. Mavis has lived by herself since Lenny died of stomach cancer a few years ago. This thief," he nodded towards the dead boy, "had already pocketed

much of Mavis's jewellery, including Lenny's George Cross, but that wasn't enough for the vicious bastard. He barged into the bedroom, waking her up, almost causing a heart attack, and kicked her to death. My wife and I heard her screams from our house, but by the time I had managed to break the door down, it was too late for the old girl. I found Mavis - an eighty-three year-old Alzheimer's sufferer – with a knitting needle stabbed in each eye. The little bastard was urinating on her as I battered my way in."
"So you hung him?"

"Not straight away. My neighbours and I conducted a fair trial."
"And you found him guilty?" Ethan asked, stunned.

"That is correct."

"And his sentence was death?"

"We believe it was the right charge."

Ethan turned when he heard retching and gagging coming from the taxi. A second later and the door was pushed open, Karris practically dragging Lincoln out, spewing the contents of his stomach over the drenched pavement. A yellow puddle of vomit, digested food marinated in lashings of stomach juice, stinking of rotten eggs and vinegar, pooled up in front of his Fireman Sam Velcro slippers. Lincoln coughed and dry-heaved; Karris gently rubbed his back, promising him he was going to be okay. Ethan went to approach his son when the shotgun was suddenly raised and aimed at Lincoln.

"You have a child with you?" said Earl. He sounded genuinely shocked, as though he had just discovered another man's car parked in his driveway. "You brought a child here?"

"He's my son," Ethan said. He craved to reach out and grab that long barrel, point it away from Lincoln, wrap the bastard around this fucker's neck, but he didn't want to make any sudden movements that he might regret. Instead, he dropped the hammer onto the saturated ground and held up his hands to prove he was no prodigious threat. Karris looked absolutely terrified.

"You need to leave right now," Earl barked. "You need to get in your car, leave, and never come back. And you need to take him with you."

"I don't have a problem with that," Ethan said. "But you need to stop pointing that gun at my boy."

"Why did you bring him here?"

"We didn't. You shot us off the bloody road. He's sick, that's all. Are you people really that far up your own arse that you can't cope with a little vomit?"

"He's infected, you bloody idiot. Have you not seen thc news?"

"I've seen all kinds of crap tonight. And much of it wasn't on a TV. My son is sick, not infected. He's probably scared shitless after having a fucking shotgun fired at him."

"No, you don't understand," Earl Topinka said. "Hold on here for a second, will you?"

"I thought you wanted us gone?"

"Please, just stay here for a second. I believe I have something you'll want to see."
"Why can't you just tell us?"

"Please, just one second." And with that he was toddling back into the darkness of morning, taking the double-barrel menace with him.
Ethan immediately crossed to Karris and kissed her rain-soaked forehead. Lincoln had stopped being sick, but he was still burning up a worryingly high temperature. Ethan handballed the rockery at the front of the cab away, and then climbed back behind the wheel of the taxi. He fired up the engine, relieved when it roared to life with the twist of the key. He reversed back onto the road, ordering Karris and Lincoln back inside. Dave remained in the pouring rain.
"Are you getting in or what, mate?" Ethan asked through the disintegrated passenger window.

"Don't you want to see what he has to show you?" Dave replied.
"I couldn't give a toss, mate. The bloke's a bloody fossil."

"But what if he's right?"

"What about, Dave?"

"What if Lincoln's infected?"

You can't be fucking serious.

"We don't have time for this right now. We need to get back to help Ma and Lee."

"I know, but..."

"What? What is there to think about, Dave?"

Before Dave could answer, Earl Topinka waded his way back across the road. He had left the shotgun indoors and he approached the droning taxi with a flashlight in one hand and a mobile phone in the other. He also had a red bandanna wrapped around his nose and mouth. He ushered Dave forward.

"Should I go?"

"I thought you wanted to see what he had?"

Dave glanced awkwardly at his youngest brother and then marched across the road. He stepped in an ankle-length puddle and dirty rainwater soaked his foot.
"The TV stopped broadcasting a few hours ago. All they're showing now is a public service announcement."

Dave nodded. "I know. We've seen it."

"Then you need to see this." Earl tossed an iPhone over to Dave who caught it as though it were a baseball. Ethan climbed out of the taxi to see what his brother was looking at.

BBC news webpage: white Transit van on fire, flames licking through the shattered windscreen, a shopping cart pushed over on its side next to the flaming combustion, a young rioter wearing a grey hooded top and a scarf covering the lower half of his face, proudly staring into the camera. Above the picture, in bold capitals, was the headline SPORADIC TROUBLE ERUPTS IN ENGLISH

CITIES – IS INFECTION TO BLAME? Ethan's eyes quickly scanned the bulletin.

Civil unrest broke out tonight in every major city in Britain with shops and even people's homes being looted and set alight. There have been as many as a thousand deaths as the police lost control of the streets to rampaging hordes and had to depend on the intervention of the military to try and restore order. The Prime Minister is due to make an announcement at 8 A.M. outside of Downing Street condemning the needless deaths, but some critics believe he should have been more active throughout the night. The Mayor of London was assassinated by a hooded menace calling himself simply Darrell, and his death has been paraded on the internet.

"We know all of this already. It's not news. Come on, Dave, let's go." "My daughter lives in New Jersey?" Earl Topinka said into the red bandanna. "She rang and told me that disturbances have been reported in America. Facebook has gone into meltdown due to the amount of people around the world reporting violence and looting in their cities. People are saying that some kind of infection is making them behave this way."

"And what does any of this have to do with my son?"

"It only infects children."

Ethan chuckled humourlessly. "Only infects children?"

"That's what the Internet is saying."

"Well, if it's on the Internet then it must be true."

"There was a hospital porter who gave an interview to a journalist claiming the government was injecting newborn babies with a fluid that had the potential to turn them into feral teenagers come puberty. I know it sounds far-fetched, but the Internet deleted the video twenty minutes after it was posted. If you search for it now, your computer downloads a virus. Why would they do that? What have they got to hide?"

"I don't have time for this bullshit." Ethan walked back to the taxi. "Dave, let's go."

Dave Hardcastle looked at his youngest brother with a flicker of shame in his eyes. "I'm sorry. I'm not coming with you."

"What? What do you mean?"

"If Lincoln's infected then I can't get in the car."

"He's not infected. He's sick. Why are you listening to this relic?"

Dave glanced over to the watery vomit on the ground. "I can't get in that car. If Lincoln's infected he could pass something onto me and I could infect Marcel when he gets back. I'm really sorry."

"Lincoln is your blood."

"I know. And I love him, you know I do, but there's something not right with him."

"What about Ma? What about Lee?"

"Go and save them. I know you can do it, Ethan."

"You're a fucking coward!"

"I know."

Ethan marched across to his brother and stopped directly in front of him, shaking his head. "I killed for you tonight."

"I'm sorry." Dave opened his arms to embrace Ethan, but the builder declined the offer, rolling his fingers into a meaty ball of knuckles, crunching it into his brother's jaw. Dave stumbled backwards, whipping around, not going down, bottom lip bloody. "Ethan, I'm so sorry."

Ethan Hardcastle nodded. "Yeah, me too, brother,"

He jumped behind the wheel and fired up the engine, roaring back home for one final confrontation.

CHAPTER 21

He stopped the taxi at the top of the driveway, not wanting to garner any unwanted attention, and pulled over on a grassy verge in front of the wooden gate. From this position, he could see that the pouring rain had completely doused the burning cars; columns of smoke still spewed into the drenched atmosphere, painting the front of his home in clouds of acidy smoke. There was a huge cloud of black smoke pumping from the back of the house, too. Ethan dreaded to think what could have caused it. He turned the vibrating engine off, pushed open the driver's door, and touched down on home soil. Lincoln was sprawled on the backseat, sleeping, but it wasn't a deep and undisturbed sleep. He had a sky-high temperature, sweating, muscle spasms and limb convulsions. In one of the winding country lanes leading back home, Karris had ordered Ethan to pull over as she peeled her son's eyelids apart to discover his pupils were dilated. He was unconscious, but his legs kicked constantly as though he was having a nightmare. His Curious George pyjamas were clammy with perspiration.

Ethan closed the driver's door as quietly as he could, and made his way to the rear of the taxi. Karris had removed her overcoat and had covered Lincoln up with it. She wrenched the side window down and poked her head through.

"You stay here with Lincoln. I'm going to make sure the house is safe."

"It seems quiet."

Ethan nodded. "I just need to make sure. If anything happens whilst I'm gone – and I mean anything – then I want you the press down on the horn, okay?"

"Okay. Be safe."

"As houses. I've left the hammer on the passenger seat."

"I love you."

"I love you, too."

Ethan stroked the side of her beautiful face with one thumb, kissed her lips, pressing urgently against each other's, tongues clashing, hands wandering, groping the same swollen area as the youth outside of kebab shop had earlier, reclaiming what was rightfully his. Karris responded with the same flustered passion, for once not complaining about his stubble or "beard-burn." Ethan reluctantly pulled away, breathless, forcing himself to break free before he jumped into the back of the cab and began removing his wife's clothing, knowing that she'd happily allow him. He stumbled awkwardly from the car, trying to ignore the pressure in his loins.

Shit, if we survive tonight, she's not going to be able to walk properly for a week.

He crunched his way down the driveway and that was when he saw dark smears on the gravel. He knew straight away it was blood. He stopped for a second, feeling as though he was being watched, hunted, and then he saw the naked body crumpled on the sodden ground.

"Lee?" he whispered to himself. He wasn't quite sure from this distance if it was his brother. "Lee? Lee, is that you, bud?" Ethan crouched down beside the blood-smeared body and rolled him over. The horrific sight reviled him; revolted him, made him want to take a scouring pad to his brain and scrub the image free. In the flutter of a heartbeat, everything changed. The Saturday night beer and Playstation ritual was gone forever; the annual "Bloke's Outing" to Margate (inspired by Del and Rodney) said Bon Voyage; the daily joke text, the weekend pint, the days out, the nights in, it was all gone in a blink of an eye. Lee Hardcastle lay dead at his feet.

He had been shot in the head at point blank range. The bullet had smashed his skull like a meteorite smashing into Earth's atmosphere; cracking bone, pulverizing teeth, embedding them into his tongue, the roof of his mouth. A puddle of blood had spread out at the back of his head with tiny islands of pink and grey brain matter dotted here and there. His lips looked like trimmings of bloodied salmon. Thankfully his eyes were closed. His face looked as though somebody had painted it bright red.
Ethan dropped onto his backside and stared in disbelief at his dead brother. He reached out and grabbed Lee's freezing cold hand. Rigor mortis had already begun to set in.

Why are you naked? What did they do to you?

A fading flame flickered inside of him. It wasn't the dwindling light of eternity, but a torturous, inconsolable flame of hatred. He wanted to destroy something beautiful. He wanted blood to stain his hands. He closed his eyes, saw the young black youth from Dave's complex, the kid he had stabbed to death, and Ethan Hardcastle smiled. He released his brother's cold hand with a sniffling kiss and roared into the surrounding darkness. The scream was inhuman, animal-like, and if it hadn't emanated from his lungs then he would have doubted the authenticity of it. He ran his fingers through the gravel, digging fingernails into hard soil, wanting to feel pain. He looked towards the dark house. He knew what he had to do.

"I'm sorry, bro," he whispered. He kissed his brother on his blood-soaked forehead, ignoring the burnt-bacon stench wafting from the cavity, and climbed to his feet, wiping tears from his eyes with the back of his hand. He unzipped his Duffle coat and pulled it off; bare arms and white vest exposed to nature's tears. He draped it over his dead brother and looked over to Harold. He was still sprawled beneath the blue tarpaulin.

"Look after him, Harry," Ethan sobbed. He then stepped up to the front door and pressed down on the handle.

The hallway was dark, empty. There was no point playing the stealth card anymore; that grief-stricken roar had been loud enough to hear in the neighbouring riot zone. He slapped on the fluorescents and groaned loudly. That troll of grief crawled from the void of his stomach and fired another arrow of sorrow into his ruptured heart. He stumbled back against the closed door.

Bella lay dead in the hallway. Her brown and white fluffy fur was now completely red and clumped together, tacky, gummy with blood. He dropped to one knee and realized the dog's throat had been slit. The beige carpet beneath her was blood-logged and his gallery of framed comic books had been trashed. He stroked Bella's stiffened fur and rose to his feet, stepping straight into the kitchen.

There was nobody in here either, but that didn't surprise him. The front of the house was swamped in blackness. He crossed to the sink without bothering with the lights and stopped, staring out of the smashed window. He could barely make out the blackened skeleton of the taxi. They should be safe up there. They were out of the way. He turned the faucet on, no longer caring if he was heard, and roughly washed his hands, feeling as though there wasn't enough soap in the world to cleanse his hands from the blood of his dead brother and dead dog. He turned the tap off and, without bothering to dry himself, pulled a steak knife out of the block on the side. He noticed the breadknife had disappeared. He walked back through the dark kitchen, holding the knife, stepping back into the smoky hall. When he had been a child, his next-door neighbour (a beastly alcoholic of a man) had fallen into vodka-induced oblivion one night and left the indoor heater on. At some point it had overheated, setting the house on fire. The old pisshead had survived (the fire-fighters responding too quickly in Ethan's opinion) and the place had gone up like a house on fire, nearly taking Ethan's with it. It had taken close to three weeks for their house to shred the stench of stale smoke. Ethan quietly wondered how long it'd take him to get the smell out of here.

He paused in the brightly-lit hall for a second and looked down at a corner table. There were two framed photographs perched on top. One was him and Dave at a fancy-dress New Year's Eve party a few years back. Dave had grown out his beard and had the whole Wolverine gimmick going on. Ethan was Rocky Balboa, complete with fake broken nose and Italian Stallion dressing gown. They had had a right laugh that night. Lee had been dressed as the Joker and had got so steamed that he had ended up brawling with a very convincing Captain Picard. The photograph beside it was Lee and Ethan at the top of a mountain in New Zealand. They had climbed it for a cancer charity. He placed one onto its glass frame and left the other proudly displayed.

Ethan looked up as a shadow spilled into the hall. A young boy of about ten stepped in front of him. Ethan gripped the handle of the steak knife tighter. The youngster – wearing a blue Nike tracksuit and trainers – had a wicked-looking red welt rising on the side of his face. He walked around Ethan's house with the cocksure arrogance of a spoiled brat from an American reality TV series. He paused upon seeing Ethan standing at the end of the hall and turned on his heels, but the builder ran forward with the speed of a Jamaican sprinter, grabbing the boy by the throat, slamming him against the wall. The boy grunted and the back of his head cracked against the wall, but he swung his fist into the side of Ethan's skull, stunning him. Ethan clenched a fist, raised his arm, but he couldn't do it. He couldn't bring himself to strike a child. No matter what these fucking degenerates had done tonight, he couldn't punch a child.

And that would be his downfall.

In the split second that Ethan hesitated, the boy uncoiled like a pissed rattlesnake, and fired his knee into Ethan's crotch. The builder grunted as though he was lifting a sack of rocks and fell far enough from the boy for him to wriggle free and run down the hallway, screaming at the top of his lungs. Ethan stumbled after him, propping himself against the wall, barely managing to grab the little fucker's hood and propelling them both through the closed door leading into the dining room. Both of Ethan's thighs ploughed painfully into the table and his weight propelled him over it, rolling him onto the floor. The boy landed in a jumble of arms, legs, and chairs. Ethan scrambled forward.

The TV mounted to the wall was still turned on, still playing on mute, replaying the same public service announcement over and over again. Ethan could not believe this was the same room that his wife had treated him to a little birthday fellatio only a few hours ago. Things had spiralled out of control so quickly. He'd forgotten it had been his birthday. He grabbed a handful of the boy's jumper and pulled him forward.
"Who killed my brother?"

"Fuck you!"

Ethan climbed from his knees to his feet and dragged the foul-mouthed boy with him, pulling him as though he had just developed cramp in a deep stretch of sea, crunching fingers into fist, stopping only when he saw the three other occupants in the room. He stared, slack-jawed, at his mother and Bryan, sitting side-by-side, gaffer tape strapped around their mouths, wrapped around their wrists, securing them to chairs. Bryan was bleeding from both nostrils, bloody-mucus bubbling, and Ethan's eyes fell upon the teenager standing behind them. He recognized him immediately as the acne-riddled terror who had called Karris a dog earlier. Ethan's fingers tightened on the little bastard as he realized there was a handgun pointed at the back of his mother's head.
"Let him go or I'll blow her fuckin' head off!"

Instinctively, Ethan loosened his grip on the boy, taking a delicate step forward. His mother was sobbing and shaking her head from side to side. Ethan silently wondered how many more tears her eyes were capable of producing.
"Let her go," Ethan said.

“Put the knife on the table,” the youth demanded.

“Ethan defiantly shook his head. “Let her go first.”

“I said put the knife on the fuckin’ table, yeah?”

“No!”

A loud crack exploded in the room, instantly followed by a blinding flash; Ethan balked backwards, stumbling into a hard-backed dining chair, almost falling flat on his back. His mother screamed high-pitched. And before it became evident that the mongrel had fired a warning shot into the ceiling, Ethan mistook raining plaster for bloody sputum. He tossed the steak knife onto the table. It glided across its polished surface and clanked against the candlestick holder.
“Next bullet goes in the back of her nut.”

“I dropped the knife. I did what you said.”

“Now let go of him.”

Ethan nodded. He couldn’t overlook the revolting feeling that a bonfire of hatred was smouldering against his pounding heart. Fingers released the catch of the day. The young boy scampered around the table, cockily readjusting his collar as he went.
Nice going, arsehole; your mother and best friend are about to be murdered because you got battered by a fucking ten-year-old boy!
“Where’s the safe?” The acne-plagued youth ambled around the dining table and slipped the serrated blade of the steak knife down the back of his jogging trousers. “What are you talking about?” Ethan Hardcastle forced

the syllables out of the dry chasm his mouth had become.

"You've got a safe, right?"

"What? Who told you this?"

"Your brother before I blew his fuckin' head off!"

Ethan forced back a sob. "You son of a bitch!"

"Where's the safe?"

"Is that what this is all about?"

"I won't ask you again."

"You killed my brother! You killed my stepfather! You killed my fucking dog!" Spittle lathered the yob's face. "You killed them all for a fucking robbery?"

"If it's any consolation you're about to join him. Now where is the safe?"

"You people may be sick. There's an infection spreading through Britain tonight. It's turning young people like you into regressive—"

The yob lunged forward before Ethan could finish pleading, aiming the centrepiece of the Beretta against his sweaty forehead, muzzle yawning, broiled gunpowder making his eyes water.

"Go on then!" Ethan blared. "Do it! What are you waiting for? Shoot me, you fucking pussy!"

The door behind him unexpectedly kicked open and another lout barged into the room. Ethan's heart lurched like a chained Rottweiler when he witnessed Karris

dragged, kicking and screaming, into the dining room. The yob holding the Beretta stepped back as his partner in crime brutally forced her against the table.
What the fuck? Where's Lincoln?

"Karris," Ethan groaned. "Karris, are you okay? Have they hurt you?" Before she could reply, he turned his attention towards the fucker with the gun. "Let her go. I'll fucking show you where the money is, but let my wife go, you coward!"
The punk who had literally just hauled Karris into the room, turned towards Ethan, glaring, eyes sceptic, dissecting the builder from beneath the peak of his baseball cap. He was wearing khaki cargo shorts and a blue polo T-shirt with the collar erect. A pair of anaemic trainers was laced to his feet, looking like they probably cost more than Ethan's house. He stepped up beside his companion.
"What's this bullshit I heard you spouting about an infection spreading through Britain?"

"It's not bullshit. I only wish it was."

"I haven't heard anything. What about you, Kieran?"

"Nah," the one called Kieran answered. "I haven't heard anythin'."
"You hear that?"

"I'm telling the truth."

"We don't believe you."

"Stretch, ask him where the safe is," Kieran said.

"Oh my fucking Lord!" Ethan cursed at the top of his lungs. "I don't know all the facts, okay? All I've heard is that an infection of some kind has spread across England – maybe the world – tonight. Like I said, I don't know much about it."
"You don't know shit," Kieran spat.

"Have you vomited tonight?" Ethan whirled around, staring directly at Kieran. "Have you had a high temperature? Have you been lethargic? Did you choose to murder two innocent people or were you overwhelmed to kill them before they killed you?"
"I haven't been sick," Kieran said. He applied and disengaged the safety on the Beretta repeatedly as he paced back and forth.
"Yeah, you have."

Kieran glared through eyes as wide as saucers at Stretch.

"We've all been sick. I've been throwing up pigs in a blanket all day."
"It's just the nutty Baby Bhang we smoked—"

"Look, if you let my wife go," Ethan said, interrupting Kieran, figuring he'd have a better chance of negotiating with the comically named Stretch, "then I will do everything within my power to stop you going to prison. You're sick. You have no control over what you're doing. Please, just let my family go."
"I've had enough of your bollocks," Kieran snarled. He pulled back on the hammer of the Beretta and aimed the muzzle once more at Ethan's head. Karris whimpered like a badly-treated puppy. Ethan glared directly into Kieran's soul. The pad of his finger brushed against the stiff trigger.

Ethan sidestepped Kieran, grabbing the gun's barrel, wrapping fingers around it, yanking Kieran forward, and blasting an elbow into his nose. He heard Karris scream feverishly, heard Kieran grunt in pain, heard his cartilage snap, and heard his mother yelling "nmm" "nmm" "nmm" into the matte black tape over her mouth. Then he felt strong hands grip his shoulders, pulling him backwards, wrenching him away from Kieran as though he was a car wreck connected to a tow truck. Ethan's hands covered his head as a volley of left and rights began pouring down.

Bryan strained every muscle in both of his arms trying to break free of the entrapment of the chair. He screamed for Karris to unfasten him, but the gaffer tape transformed his pleas into frenzied panic. Belinda was crying again; mascara, snot, lathering her face, looking like pond water algae. Ethan tried to reach for her, but Stretch clung to him like a Velociraptor; biting, clawing, leaving Ethan no other choice but to turn, grabbing Stretch by the waist, interlocking fingers, lifting, pushing into the human blocking sled, throwing the weasel across the table. The punk landed flat on his back with a loud crash.

Ethan turned and grabbed a handful of zit-face's greasy mop, yanking him away from the Beretta, spinning him, smashing the joint of his knee into the fucker's stomach, crashing an elbow to the back of his neck. Kieran collapsed to the floor. He turned like a medieval killing machine, just managing to snatch a glimpse of the ten year-old boy charging forwards and roaring, before reflex thwarted morals, and he hit the boy under the chin with a perfect uppercut. The boy went down. He didn't move.
Ethan (now on a roll) turned, managed to grab Kieran's ankle before he could crawl to the Beretta, but forgot about the steak knife. Kieran jerked it free and carved at

Ethan's forearm as though it were a juicy hog roast; slashing, cutting, tearing, jaggedly ripping open Ethan's arm, blood pouring free. Ethan roared like a grieving lioness, falling away, landing on his back, clamping his good hand to the wound, temporarily stemming the flow, but aware that only a nurse with a degree in embroidery would be able to stop the gush. Stretch scrambled around the table towards him and Ethan jumped into his boots to meet him. Bryan pushed himself and the chair he was strapped to away from the table, his shoulder catching Stretch in the ribs, slapping him against the wall. The wooden stilts beneath the chair snapped, forcing both men to the floor. Bryan, at an obvious disadvantage with his hands still coupled to the chair, managed to find a sprinkling of that luck he had always been blessed with, and landed on top of Stretch. The gaffer tape was torn free. Teeth quickly sank into the carbuncle of flesh his deltoid offered, biting down hard, drawing blood, white pearls turning red.

Kieran grabbed Ethan and spun him, throwing a punch that the builder was quick to duck, and he grabbed Kieran, pulling him forward, groping fingers wrapping around his throat, squeezing. Kieran still had plenty of fight in him, though, gripping his archenemy in a chokehold of his own. Both men crushed the other's oesophagi, squashing air from deflating lungs.

And then – more defining than Eliot Ness calling up his Untouchables or Yul Brynner hiring six Magnificent gunslingers, more overriding than even the Duke kissing Maureen O'Hara in a rain-scorched graveyard or Charlton Heston catching a hint of liberation poking from a shoreline – the words "Take your hands off of my son!" poured into the dining room. And Ethan watched, mesmerised, as a blood-smeared Harold Singleton stumbled into the doorway. The Beretta was gripped in one shaky hand.

CHAPTER 22

Ethan actually managed to smile.

Belinda looked like she hadn't just seen a ghost. She looked as though the phantom wraith of her broken heart had returned just in time to stop her youngest son being kicked to death.

"Harry," Ethan hissed. His hands were still clasped to Kieran's throat.
Bryan rolled to one side and whispered for Karris to untie him. Karris didn't move. She didn't even hear him.

Kieran ignored the bleeding relic in the doorway, renewing his efforts, trying to get the better of Ethan.

"I said take your hands off of my son!" Harold bellowed. He staggered drunkenly into the dining room. One hand held the Beretta; the other clutched the bloody crater in the back of his head. It looked as though somebody had dyed his Hawaiian shirt dark red. "I won't tell you again."

Ethan Hardcastle gawked into the two hate-fuelled eyes of his nemesis. He couldn't stop the cocky smile creasing over his stubbly features. "You heard the man."
"No, Ethan. I'm talking to you."

The words were fucking dreadful.

And it was then – realization creeping up on his repelled brain like a Greek army stealthily attacking the sleeping Trojans – Ethan noticed the Beretta was pointed at him for a third time that night.

"Take your hands off of my son, Ethan."

"Your son," The words sounded like air trapped in a pipe. "He's your son?"
"That's right." Harold limped into the room, walking as though he had space boots on, and aimed the Beretta at Ethan. He held out his other hand to Kieran. Horrified, Ethan watched the youth as he was plucked free of his grasp; he stepped up beside his father. Obnoxiously, he brushed Ethan's fingerprints from of the front of his coat. "They're both my boys." He nodded his head towards Stretch. He was still sitting on the floor with his back against the wall, clutching his shoulder. There was a bloody spot courtesy of Bryan's gnashing fangs.

"Who's he?" Ethan nodded towards the unconscious boy.

"Jordan? He's my nephew."

"What do you mean?" Ethan shook his head, refusing to believe what he was hearing. He looked over to his sobbing mother. "What's he talking about, Ma?"

She shook her head and closed her eyes. Karris crossed to her and removed the gag, snapping the adhesive tape, freeing her hands. She rose unsteadily to her feet, standing like she was on the deck of a fishing boat caught in the perfect storm.
"Hey, princess," Harold said, glancing across to Belinda. "I'm sorry you had to find out this way."

"Oh, Harold!" she shouted, pushing freed hands through her shoulder-length hair. A combination of sweat and hair lacquer made it appear as though she was wearing Something about Mary hair gel.

"What are you talking about? These are very bad people."

"No, Belinda, love. They're misunderstood, that's all."

"Misunderstood?" Ethan placed his hands on the table and hung his head. A bloody handprint smeared the smooth oak. "Harry, they almost beat you to death."
"I know." He glanced across to Kieran. "You did go a little too far."
"You said make it look realistic."

Harold smiled that crooked smile. "How can I argue with that? Where's your sister?"
Belinda howled; her voice a monochrome of disbelieving guilt.
"She didn't make it. They killed her." Kieran pointed an accusatory finger across the table at Belinda. "She killed her."
"What the hell're you talking about, son?"

"Charlotte's dead, yeah? She stabbed her."

Harold reeled against the wall. He lowered the Beretta as the death of his daughter soaked into his shocked brain. He rubbed a grubby hand across his bloodshot eyes, swiping tears away. A puddle of blood painted his shadow vivid red.
"You..." his voice broke, cracked, and failed him. "You killed my little girl?"
"They killed my son."

"We thought they'd killed you, too," Ethan added.

"Unfortunately not," Bryan remarked.

“Shut up!” Harold roared. “I’m talking to her!”

“Well that’s tough shit.” Ethan said. “Why don’t you tell us about tonight, Harry?”
Harold disregarded Ethan with a wave of the gun. He turned towards Kieran. “Are you sure she’s dead?”

Zit-face nodded his head. “Died right in my arms, didn’t she?”
“Did you get it?”

“Not yet. The pussy was about to tell me where it is before the shit hit the fan.”
“Has he got what?” Ethan challenged.

“Did you check the cellar?” Harold enquired.

Ethan stepped directly in front of Harold. “Has he got what?”
He looked from Harold to Kieran to Stretch to Jordan. And the penny finally dropped.
Please return your seat backs to their full upright and locked position. “You son of a bitch,” Ethan smiled humourlessly. “Tonight was a setup. You were in on it from the beginning, weren’t you?”
“What do you mean?” Karris asked from over his bloody shoulder.
“It was a setup. The whole fucking thing was a setup.”

“What!?”

“Tell them, Harry.” Ethan stepped over the unconscious Jordan and right in his stepfather’s face. “Tell them. Tell them how everything from you being knocked out to us believing you were dead was a setup."

"I don't understand," Belinda croaked from the back of the room. "What has any of this got to do with my Lee?"

"Absolutely nothing," Ethan answered. "It has nothing to do with Lee. It's about money. It's about the money in my safe. It's about the weekly takings, right?"

"I needed to make it look convincing," Harold explained. He pulled a chair out and slumped into it. Blood trickled down his face and beat a rhythmical tattoo against the dining table. "Nobody was supposed to get hurt. That's the truth. You were meant to get scared a little, but that's all."

"How long have you been planning this?" Belinda asked. She was sobbing again now into another paper handkerchief. "How long have you been planning to rob my son?"

"I've had my eye on this place for a few months. You know what your mother's like; can't keep her frigging mouth shut. She told me you had a bulging safe somewhere in here. I never had an opportunity to find out where you kept it. Then the riots happened—"

"And you hit the jackpot."

Harold nodded.

"Harold," Ethan breathed. "I have something to tell you. There is no safe. Not here, anyhow. Do you really think I'd keep a safe full of money in my house with you lurking about?"

"He's lyin'!" Kieran bellowed. "He's got to be!"

"Am I? Well go ahead and tear this place apart. Rip the fucking floors up. You won't find anything."

"Then where is it?" growled Harold.

"Nathan's house, you bloody moron. It's at my business partner's."
Harold kicked back the chair and jumped to his feet. "It doesn't change the fact you killed my little girl."

"That whore killed my son!" Belinda screeched. Fists pounded her chest as if she were an enraged primate. "I'm glad she's dead! Her body's back there! And I hope she rots in hell!"

Harold Singleton roared unintelligibly and pointed the gun at his fiancée, pulling back the trigger, firing off a round. Ethan kicked out half a second before the bullet propelled from the chamber, and the Beretta was swatted aside, racing bullet going wide, crashing through the bay window. Rain and wind swept into the dining room. Harold lost all remaining control and pistol-whipped Ethan across the face. The blunt end of the Beretta made fierce contact with his mouth. Front teeth were loosened. Ethan fell to the ground, blood spilling from smashed lips. Bryan stepped forward, but Stretch and Kieran both leapt on him, dwarfing his body, forcing the lawyer down, pinning him beneath their combined weight. Belinda screamed uselessly.
"I've had enough of you, you little shit," Harold spat. The words sounded like phlegmy gravel being stepped on. "You never liked me, did you? You always looked down your nose at me. Thought you had it all, didn't you? A nice house, a beautiful son, heir to the family business, money in the bank, a gorgeous wife, you were fucking

made! You thought that you were better than me. You thought I would never have any of that."

"And I was right. You had to steal it. But you couldn't even get that right."
"The money was plan A. Now it's time for plan B. You've made this fucking personal, you little prick. I want something now that's only yours." He looked across to Karris. "Now I want her!"

CHAPTER 23

Ethan Hardcastle tried to speak, but the combination of a parched mouth and the serrated blade of the steak knife pressing against his thyroid cartilage prevented it. He could feel fetid breath on the back of his neck. He knew Kieran wouldn't think twice about slashing his throat if his father demanded. He tried to step forward. Kieran yanked his head back and applied even more pressure to the blade.

Bryan was in a similar quandary. Stretch had forced him onto his stomach, bloody nose curled into the thick weave of the carpet, hands clasped behind his head, the Beretta trained on him. Every time he inhaled, dust mites filled his swollen nostrils.

Harold grabbed Karris by the elbow and dragged her across to the table. He tried bending her over it, but didn't take into account the fighting spirit of Karris Hardcastle. She'd been a victim all of her life; victim of weight, victim of bullying, victim of depression, and she was determined not to become a victim of rape as well. She arched her back, kicked her legs, and scratched long fingernails down Harold's jowls. A weighty backhander to her face put an end to that nonsense.

"Fuck," Kieran chuckled into Ethan's ear. "He almost slapped her mouth down to her arse."

Molars chewed manically on the inside of his mouth. Ethan closed his eyes. He could still hear screaming, pleading, begging, and he opened them in time to see Harold groping her rump. Ethan opened his mouth to roar, but thousands of threats became a log-jam in his larynx. He closed it again. "Hey," Harold gasped, looking towards Stretch, crooking a thumb towards Belinda. "Make sure she watches the show."

Do something you fucking prick!

Harold pulled Karris towards him and ripped open her white blouse, buttons falling like pearled snowflakes. He grabbed at her huge breasts, snatching them, squeezing, pushing filthy fingers under her lace bra, kneading nipples, mounding soft flesh. He bit and sucked noisily at her neck. Karris closed her eyes, feeling horrible eager fingers unbuttoning her jeans. Belinda retched, vomited all over the dining room floor.
Harold ignored his fiancée and yanked Karris's jeans down past her thighs, revealing the red thong covering her womanhood, pushing the denims down, twisting them around her knees, stopping their descent, a temporary pit-stop with the finishing line in sight.

"Please, don't do this, Harold," Karris appealed. Even as she spoke, she could feel his erection pressing against her leg. "You don't have to."
"No, you're right," Harold breathed. Trembling fingers unbuckled the belt from around his waist. His breath smelt like sewer gas. "I don't have to. I want to."
"No, please, Harold—"

He gagged her with his hand. "I've always had a thing for you. Did you know that? Of course you did. That's why you'd always wear short skirts and get dolled up when you knew I was coming over. Did you get a thrill out of that? Did you get a thrill infuriating an old dinosaur like me?"
Karris shook her head. Tears spilled down her flushed cheeks.
"Did you know that, Ethan?" Harold bellowed. Rough hands seized her hips. "Did you know she had a thing for me?"

Ethan opened his mouth.

The knife pressed firmer against his throat.

Belinda groaned loudly.

Forearm pressed against the base of the neck, and Karris was pushed roughly over the dining table, one hand pulling at her thong, ripping the flimsy material away, exposing tanned stretch marks. The other hand released his erect member and positioned him behind her bare buttocks. With one gloating look at Belinda, Harold Singleton pushed deep inside of Karris. A sudden sharp pain made her scream, head down, hair falling over her beautiful face, fingernails scratching against the smooth surface of the table. He began to thrust his hips as he entered deeper. Her belly erupted in flames of agony. She called out for Ethan to help.
Do something, you fucking coward! He's raping your wife!
Ethan tried to look away from the savagery, look at the floor, the wall, anywhere, but the shit behind him grabbed Ethan by his fringe and jerked his head back. He tried closing his eyes but the image of Harold pounding against Karris's backside plagued him. He blinked them open, realizing from the position Harold was in, combined with the painful wails of Karris, that she was being violated in such a way that not even he had dared to consider. Apart from the occasional dirty joke or drunken safari, her anal passage was strictly off-limits.

Ethan balled up his fists.

And the dining room door crashed open. The wooden partition bounced off the wall, catching Kieran completely off-guard, and Lincoln charged into the room, breathing raggedly, looking like a wild dog cornered by a circle of humans. Ethan reacted immediately. He didn't bother to wonder what had urged his son to barge into the room and he refused to waste time thinking about why he looked so feral. The word INFECTION flitted through his brain, of course, but it genuinely was a whisper in the wind. He saw his one and only chance and he was going to snatch it with both hands. He fired the elbow of his injured arm into Kieran's throat, the impact hard, bruising tissue, and grabbed the wrist holding the knife, twisting it. He heard the bone snap, quickly followed by the sound of the blade land on the floor. He managed to grab a snatch of Lincoln before Kieran crunched them both against the wall. He shoved the youth aside and watched Lincoln leap forward, using the back of Harold's legs as a launch pad, and scramble up his spine. The unexpected weight of the infant made Harold fall away from the boy's screaming mother. Baby teeth sank into Harold's trapezius muscle. Blood gouged down Lincoln's throat.

Jesus Christ!

Bryan quickly took advantage of the anarchy unfolding and grabbed Stretch by the throat, pushing him up, driving a fist into the bridge of his nose. The youth cried out in pain and fell away. Bryan rolled onto his side, galloping on hands and knees underneath the dining table just as the evil bastard fired the Beretta. The bullet obliterated the wooden leg holding the table up, the entire thing lopsided, falling at a ninety degree angle, giving Bryan more cover.

"Bryan!" Ethan roared.

“What?”

“Are you okay?”

“We need to get the fuck out of here!”

“I know. You head towards the door. I’m going for Karris and Ma.”
Ethan crept around the table and leapt at Stretch, taking him by surprise. He charged into him and introduced his knee to the lad’s crotch. The youth slid down the wall, wailing in agony, holding his maltreated manhood, but before Ethan could make for his wife, Harold barged into him. He was clutching the steak knife in one bloody hand, raising it above his head, ready to strike, but suddenly Lincoln was cuddling his leg as though Lennie had just been handed a living mouse, and bit into Harold’s inner thigh. A mouthful of denim and flesh was torn away. Harold yowled in pain and tried to dispatch the child from his leg. He doubled over; crying, screaming, threatening, and the workhorse hands of Ethan Hardcastle grabbed him, revenge becoming a four-knuckled word.

Ethan shouted for Karris to get out of the house.

“What about you?”

“I’ll be right behind you. I’m just grabbing Lincoln.”

His semi-conscious stepfather had landed perched against the lopsided tabletop. Ethan crouched in front him and placed a bloody hand on Lincoln’s hunched shoulders. As soon as the contact was made with the five year-old boy – the same five-year-old boy he had taught to ride a bike, build a cushion-fort in the front room, had read The Tiger

Who Came to Tea to a million times, wrestled with, and kicked a football with – he evaporated. Instead of allowing his father's arms to embrace him, Lincoln charged forward, blood-drenched jaws snapping for Ethan's throat. He fell backwards and his racing brain refused to accept that his son, his flesh and blood, had just tried inflicting physical harm upon another person. He scrabbled backwards on heels and elbows. An overturned chair provided the blockage required to stop Lincoln reaching his intended target.
Karris pushed herself over the table and hopped towards his mother. Apart from the red thong and bra, she was stark naked. She reached Belinda and pulled her jeans up, fastening them, before taking the older woman by the hand and pulling her towards the dining room door. Belinda refused to budge. Words were exchanged. Ethan couldn't hear what. Then Belinda walloped Karris across her bruised face. The whole scene played out in Rocky-slow-motion. Ethan, shocked, stepped forward just as Kieran pounced again. Both men hit the dining table, Ethan managing to toss the vile youth aside.

"What are you doing, Ma?"

"She's a slut!"

"He was lying."

"No! He is a good man!

Karris laughed hysterically. "He just fucking raped me!"

"I saw it with my own eyes, Ethan. This girl's a jezebel!"

And then the bay window imploded with a deafening krrssshhhh and an invading phantasmagoria of groping hands and rain-slicked fingers surged into the room. They immediately wrapped around the old woman and dragged her out into the thundery morning. He heard her screaming his name. He heard her begging for help. And then he heard her no more.

A stream of hooded youths poured through the glass-toothed orifice. Stretch staggered forward and Ethan sailed a fist into the bastard's jaw. He turned towards the doorway, looking desperately at Bryan and Karris, the biggest dilemma of his life beating the hell out of him.

Do I get out now or go back? I can't even see Ma and I doubt Lincoln even recognize me?

But then the heartbreaking decision was made for him as the rampaging horde scrambling through the broken window pinned Harold by his arms and legs against the partially collapsed table, a barrage of hooded children stomping and kicking him, turning over chairs, splintering legs free, beating him with makeshift batons.

"Help me!" Harold shouted. He looked pleadingly towards Ethan. "Help me, please!"

Ethan stepped forward.

Karris pulled him back. "Don't even think about it."

"They're going to kill him."

"Good."

Harold yelped as something cold, hard, and serrated plunged into his stomach. White stars floated in front of his eyes as air was evicted from skewered lungs. Blood-slicked fingers reached for the handle of the steak knife, his search only revealing the clenched fist of the stabber. Bloodshot eyes reported to a concussed brain the identity of the person that had just turned him into human coleslaw. Then the knife was yanked free, making a wet sucking sound, and Kieran Singleton brought it plunging down again and again and again.

CHAPTER 24

Ethan closed the door and quickly looked around for something to barricade it with. Apart from the corner table (which they would easily dispose of) there was nothing. Karris, wearing only jeans and a barely containable bra, reached for the door handle. Ethan grabbed her by the shoulders.
"Lincoln is in there!"

Ethan could taste his heart at the back of his throat. "There's nothing we can do for him."

"What do you mean?" Karris cried, shrugging his hands free. "He's my son!"
"No, he's not. Not anymore."

A fist clattered against the opposite side of the door.

Bryan nervously licked his lips. "What are you talking about, Eth?"
"He's changed."

"Changed?" Bryan asked, dumbfounded.

"He's changed into one of them, Karris. Earl Topinka was telling the truth. An infection or a virus or something is changing all of the children. We have to get away from here."

There was another crash against the door. Wood splintered.
"Wait a minute," Bryan said. He unzipped his navy jacket and draped it around Karris's trembling shoulders,

reinstating her dignity. "What infection? I heard you say something in there, but I just thought you were bargaining."
More fists rebounded off the door. He could feel the handle twisting untiringly in his grip. He heard Harold screaming, screaming as though Edvard Munch was doing a self-portrait.
They'll be out soon! There's nothing to stop them!

"Bryan, I don't have time for a discussion. Go into the front room, see if you can find anything to prise this bloody door closed with."
Before the stick-thin lawyer could move, something smashed through the door; something small but zooming at around 1100 feet per second, blasting a whole roughly the size of a fist into the door. Before Ethan Hardcastle recognized the chaperoning crack of the gunshot, a hollow tipped bullet ploughed into his shoulder, pulverizing flesh, fender-bending bone, throwing Ethan flat on his back. His head ricocheted off the cord carpet. Fried flesh, fragmented bone, dregs of blood sprayed the opposite wall.
"Ethan!" Karris shrieked.

It felt as though somebody had thrust freezing cold iron tongues into his shoulder, numbing from the peak of his shoulder all the way down to the tip of his middle finger. His forearm had already been mangled by the steak knife earlier, but now the whole limb was deadweight. He was bleeding badly. His vest had turned completely dark maroon. Breathlessly, he tried to climb to his feet, but the trauma had turned his legs to jelly. He fell back down on the floor.
"Ethan!" Bryan roared, creeping forward. "I'm coming, mate."

“No!” Ethan held up one blood-soaked hand to bring his friend to a standstill. “Don’t come any closer. There’s a taxi at the top of the driveway. Get yourself and Karris far away from here!”
“No,” Karris babbled. “I’ll bring the car around the front. You get Ethan to his feet and meet me on the driveway.”

“Karris—”

“This isn’t up for a debate. They’ll be out soon.”

As though right on cue, the dining room door was kicked open and two hooded youths about fourteen years-old barged into the corridor, sprinting towards them. Ethan gritted his teeth and forced himself to his feet. Bryan grabbed the first Neanderthal by the scruff of his coat and punched him straight in the mouth, cursing as the second jumped on his back, forcing both of them to the floor. Carpet burns shredded his chin. Bryan drove the point of his elbow into something soft, heard the gruff moan of distress, and shrugged him free. Two more tried clambering free of the mobocracy in the dining room. Ethan kicked the door closed, bolting it with his own body.
“Karris, get outta here!”

The door thrust open.

Ethan slammed it closed with his good shoulder. When he looked back, his wife had vanished. The front door was wide open.
Thank God!

Another gunshot blasted through the door. This one was at head height and narrowly missed Ethan by inches. He roared in both fear and pain. And then the door was forced open completely.

The menace standing on the opposite side, slick with blood, eyes wide, steak knife cemented in his grasp, stepped forward. Ethan backed away as Kieran Singleton marched towards him, tip of the blade dripping with Harold's blood. Ethan turned and ran into the kitchen; Kieran in hot, blood-famished, pursuit.

Bryan tried for the front door. An advancing legion of hooded morons blew like a hurricane into the corridor, cutting him off, leaving him no choice than to run in the opposite direction. He raced into the front room and flung open the back doors, galloping through the skeleton of the conservatory and sprinting towards the back fence leading onto the moors. The atmosphere was thick with smoke from the downed military helicopter. It filled his lungs, clogged the back of his throat, made his eyes stream, but he refused to slow down. Any moment now, the bastards would be on him. They'd kill him. He had no doubt about that.

The rain was falling heavily from roiling thunderheads; falling in saturating sheets, drenching him, making clothes stick to his body. The pouring rain made a hissing noise. It reminded him of that nature documentary Aiko used to watch on National Geographic.

Belinda's corpse was sprawled in the middle of the lawn, bloody, beaten, soaking, looking like roadkill left for Mother Nature to nibble on. Her right arm had been removed and left a few paces in front of her body. Blood turned dewy grass slushy. He didn't stop. He pumped his arms faster, he stretched his legs wider, but he did not stop. He slammed into the mesh face-first, grunting with pain, immediately scaling the slippery divider and dropping recklessly to freedom. He paused for the briefest of moments to catch his breath. In that interlude he saw thirteen or fifteen hooded misfits giving chase across the lawn. Their ages ranged from children to teenagers to mini-adults.

Lightning flashed.
Thunder roared.

Bryan heard the parp of a car horn from the front of the bungalow. It looked as though Karris had reached the taxi and was signalling for departure. Envious fingers rolled into tight fists. He would not be able to make it around the front of the house without getting seen. An army of bellowing kamikazes were already climbing the fence, jumping hardheartedly into obliqueness, spitting, threatening. His chances of getting out of here in that taxi were more than slim – they were fucking anorexic! He turned and cast a lingering glance over the dark moorlands stretching in front of him. Fervent wind blasted through inky tree-shaped walls, wailing in and out of distorted trunks. The gales were perfumed with the vile stench of wood rot. Branches creaked. Twisted coils of bruise-yellow appeared in the black horizon. Birdsong filled his ears. It wouldn't be long before dawn broke.

He swallowed hard and scrambled across the gurgling creek, slipping on peat-smeared rockery, splashing through icy water, grabbing tufts of grass, tree roots, hauling free, rolling through high stinging nettles, wincing as they nipped at his hands and face, attacking like mini Triffids, cursing loudly, crashing free, galloping across the moors as fast as his aching legs could carry him. By the time the first pair of tawdry trainers landed on the opposite side of the fence, Bryan had been devoured by black wilderness.

Yes, Bryan Locke really was a lucky son of a bitch.

Ethan Hardcastle, however, was not made from the same cloth. He used to joke that he was "so unlucky that if I ever fell in a barrel of tits I'd come up sucking my own thumb" or "if I ever got stranded in a desert I'd probably drown to death," but he had never actually believed it. He had never got more than three lottery numbers on a single ticket, yes, and everything he owned he'd grafted his backside off for. But that didn't mean a gypsy curse had been hexed on him, did it? He didn't even believe in things like that. However, one gunshot wound and a hacked forearm later, Ethan was seriously considering where he ranked on the Unluckiest Man in the World graph. He was leaning over the kitchen sink and looking through the smashed kitchen window, bleeding like a stuck pig. He spat a mouthful of yellowy sputum into the steel basin and saw it was flecked with redness. He turned, resting his frame against the marble work surface, and searched desperately for some kind of a weapon. Kieran barged arrogantly into the kitchen, steak knife glinting despite the lack of light. Ethan noticed the youth had pulled his hood back up.

"Wait a minute," Ethan pleaded. He realized he was trapped. He could try and escape through the shattered kitchen window, but he knew Kieran would be on him like a shark smelling blood. Wind howled into the kitchen. He could hear rain drumming against the burnt wrecks. "Just wait a minute, yeah?"
"Wait a minute? Did anybody wait a minute before they killed Charlotte?"
Ethan tried to swallow, but it was impossible. His throat was syrupy with blood. "I don't...I don't know. I wasn't here when she died."

"I was!" Kieran snapped. "Trust me, nobody gave her a chance!"
He stepped forward and raised the knife.

Ethan had one hand left to play. If it wasn't a straight flush it'd be a bloody gush.
"Why did you kill Harold?"

Kieran stopped. The knife froze above his head.

"He was your dad. A fucking pathetic excuse for one, granted, but still your dad." Every second that crawled past was a struggle to keep his knees from buckling. "Why did you kill your dad?"

"He wasn't my dad, yeah? He was one of you!"

"When he first came into the room you didn't attack him. You didn't try to kill him. Please help me to understand. My son turned tonight and I need to know why."
Kieran clenched his teeth together.

"Why didn't you attack him straight away? Why did you wait until the others turned up?" He glanced over to the folded table where the buffet had been displayed earlier. A conveyor belt of cold sausage rolls and congealed chickens drumsticks ran unappetisingly alongside each other. Nestled in between a jar of pickled onions and the bottles of cordial he saw the unlikeliest of weapons. He needed to keep this charade up and get over there.

Bright light flooded in through the broken windows of the kitchen and the unmistakable racket of a taxi engine approaching submerged the bungalow. Ethan was desperate to scream for Karris to pull over and reverse, to

get the hell out of here, but he needed to keep his poker face. He moved slowly to the left. Kieran didn't even notice. He was too busy looking out of the window at the crawling vehicle. Surprise registered in those dark irises and Ethan slipped completely in front of the buffet table, good hand searching blindly for his deterrent. Karris beeped the horn and pulled up at the fifty yard line in the driveway.
"That's your bitch, right?" Kieran said. He was pointing the blade towards the glassless window.

"Forget her," Ethan growled. "Tell me what happened in there. Tell me what made you change into this." Trembling fingertips skittered over hardened sandwiches, half-mooned pork pies, pots of coleslaw, and – aha — finally made contact with the plastic container he blindly sought.
"Nothin' turned me into anythin'," Kieran growled. He grabbed a handful of the builder's bloody vest and jerked him forward. "I'm this way through choice!"
Ethan could hear shouting emanating from the hallway and straight away he knew he was in a world of trouble. He rolled his eyes and became certain that he must have committed bigamy on Lady Luck in a previous life.

Through the doorway, Ethan saw at least a dozen breathless beasts stomp. He caught a snippet of Stretch and the Beretta, and knew time was up. They would lynch him and do worse to Karris.

Do something! Do something now!

The tip of the steak knife dripped blood.

Harold's blood!

Ethan grabbed hold of the plastic container behind his back and quickly emptied its contents on the tablecloth. A couple rolled unnoticeably onto the floor. He scooped up a handful.

The knife plunged down.

Ethan's hand drove up a fraction of a second earlier.

Kieran howled in pain and grabbed his throat, dropping the knife onto the floor. Ethan knew he had to act fast, and forced himself across the room, breathing raggedly, slamming the door closed on the hooded youths, grabbing the corner of the refrigerator, hauling it over onto its side, spilling its contents, bringing it to a rest against the bottom of the kitchen door like a metal draught excluder for a giant. He staggered back as fists pounded the door. He turned towards Kieran.

A fistful of cocktail sticks thrust under the chin was never going to keep the bastard down, but it was enough to invoke a respite from any man – even a feral maniac like him. Kieran grabbed his bloody chin and reached for the knife. Ethan charged forward and drove his knee into Kieran's shoulder. The impact slammed both men against the sink.

He heard more demanding commands for the door to be opened by the cronies in the hallway and a combined effort to shove open the door proved fruitless against the weight of the fridge. The Beretta was fired. Wood splintered.

Kieran pushed Ethan away and crashed a clenched fist into Ethan's nose. It broke in one punch. Blood trickled like runny yolk from his nostrils. A sharp pain exploded in his ribs, creasing him, flat-lining across his chest. Ethan actually felt the blade of the knife being retrieved from between his ribs. He roared and fell awkwardly against the worktops. Before his pain-ravaged brain was capable of realizing he'd been stabbed, a foul gust of stale oxygen leaked from his punctured lung, gushing up his gullet like wind up a chimney. Thick gouts of blood eagerly drowned it out and spilled from between glistening lips. Ethan could actually feel his heart clock in for overtime. He didn't know how much more his body could sustain.

The taxi beeped again. He heard the door open and the sound of a foot falling into gravel.

"No, Karris, stop!" Ethan yelled. "Get out of here now!"

Karris paused and frowned at the pale face at the disintegrated window. She saw him; bloody, pain racked, eyes wide, mouth open, and then an arm wrapped around him and yanked him into blackness. Ethan collapsed on his hands and knees, crawling immediately away, blood drooling goutily from the cavities in his shoulder and ribs, leaving puddles of it blemishing the laminate. He collapsed on his back and choked on bloody phlegm.

"Kieran, are you okay?" Stretch called through wood.

"Yeah," Kieran breathed. He placed a foot on Ethan's chest and applied pressure. Ethan grunted from between clenched teeth. "Go get the bitch from outside. I want to finish what Dad started."

"No!" Ethan swept Kieran's legs off the floor with a swipe of his good arm; screaming with the pain it produced, knocking him flat on his back, driving the air from his lungs much like the steak knife had driven it from Ethan's. He forced himself onto his knees and grabbed two handfuls of Kieran's hair, smashing the side of his head against the washing machine just as he heard the front door being opened. Ethan refused to let go and instead climbed to unsteady feet, bouncing the side of Kieran's face off the worktop. Kieran groaned and dropped to his knees. A snapped tooth surfed a wave of blood out of his mouth.

A jumble of threats and shouts came from the driveway. He looked through the glassless window and watched an army of monstrosities charge towards the taxi, illuminated by the one remaining headlamp. They were being led by Lincoln!

Ethan pulled the cutlery drawer open, the wooden handle connecting abruptly with Kieran's ear, and as the lad fell forward he tried stopping himself by reaching for the washing machine. A gloved hand slipped inside the drum and Ethan quickly kicked the door closed, breaking two fingers. Kieran screamed as though he was in the final stages of male childbirth. Ethan staggered to the stove and turned on all four hobs. Gas hissed free, filling the small kitchen, the overwhelming atoms clogging his nostrils and drying his mouth, Warning bells alerted an ignorant brain.

Karris jumped back behind the steering wheel and reversed zig-zaggedly up the driveway, slamming on the brakes and screeching to a stop. The vehicle remained motionless for a brief second as the impromptu goodbyes between husband, wife and child were exchanged. And then the taxi was put into gear and wheels chewed gravel as Karris Hardcastle galloped down the country lane.

Only one thing left to do now!

Ethan allowed a flicker of a smile to flash across his waxy face. “Hey!” Ethan bellowed at the top of his one inflatable lung. “I’m over here, you fucking arseholes!”
The mob in the driveway turned at the sound of his voice and charged towards the house. An avalanche of hoods and balaclavas and tracksuits poured through the window and pounced into the kitchen. Ethan backed away, holding his bleeding ribs. His head was spinning due to a combination of the toxic fumes and the hellfire burning in his shoulder and side. Breathing had become laborious.

“Come on,” he wheezed. “Come on.”

The kitchen heaved with youths, looking like a frat party gone bad, and at the front of the baying crowd was Lincoln. His eyes were fixed on his father, filled with hatred. He showed no remorse, no emotion. He didn’t even seem to smell the gas or ponder why his father had just called out to them. All he cared about was ripping Ethan’s face off.
Lincoln stepped forward. The crowd followed.

Ethan reached the already open cutlery drawer and snatched a handful of cutlery free. He then opened the microwave door and bunged the lot inside, twisting the dial, cranking up the wattage. There was an immediate gurgling sound like a bad stomach and then a pop-pop-popping sound as the metal acted like an antenna and bounced energy. Plumes of acrid smoke drifted from the back of the microwave.
The crowd took another step forward. Ethan backed against the wall as Stretch pulled Kieran to his feet and handed the Beretta over to his brother. Kieran gratefully

accepted it and pointed it directly at Ethan. A flash of flame licked the inside of the microwave door.

"You're dead," Kieran growled.

Ethan smiled cockily. "Me and you both,"

He closed his eyes, saw Karris, saw Lincoln, revisited his wedding day, happy days, days at the beach, teaching Lincoln to fish, running manically through lapping water, Bella chasing, Lincoln laughing. His mind hurtled back to first glances, first dates, first kisses, and then the DeLorean sped everything up, showed childbirth, Lincoln's first Christmas, dressed as an Elf, Karris laughing wholeheartedly, he saw everything, all at once, one final time before the microwave exploded and he saw no more.

James Jobling

Biography

James Jobling has always loved to write horror fiction, but National Emergency is his first piece of completed work. He is married to his Angel on his Shoulder, and has two adorable, sleep-avoiding children. He lives in Stockport, Manchester, and can be contacted through either Facebook or Twitter.

He grew up addicted to legendary horror masters such as Stephen King, Clive Barker, Shaun Hutson, Dean Koontz, and of course, James Herbert. He was fortunate enough to stumble upon a previously unheard of novel called HATER by David Moody, and rapidly became lost and submerged in this incredibly gifted writer's novels and series. He then discovered a Facebook forum dedicated to all-thing's-Moody, and it was here that he found literally hundreds of talented authors and film makers who not only had what it takes to succeed in their personal endeavours, but also had the time and patience to listen and reply to a tsunami of questions from a brand-spanking-newbie like himself who just wanted to write a story.

42158313R00137

Made in the USA
Charleston, SC
18 May 2015